MARMALADE ATKINS ON THE BALL

Also by Andrew Davies

Conrad's War
Educating Marmalade
Marmalade Atkins in Space
Marmalade Atkins' Dreadful Deeds
Marmalade Hits the Big Time

MARMALADE ATKINS ON THE BALL

by Andrew Davies

DUTTON

DUTTON

Published by the Penguin Group
Penguin Books Ltd, 27 Wrights Lane, London W8 5TZ, England
Penguin Books USA Inc., 375 Hudson Street, New York, New York 10014, USA
Penguin Books Australia Ltd, Ringwood, Victoria, Australia
Penguin Books Canada Ltd, 10 Alcorn Avenue, Toronto, Ontario, Canada M4V 3B2
Penguin Books (NZ) Ltd, 182-190 Wairau Road, Auckland 10, New Zealand

Penguin Books Ltd, Registered Offices: Harmondsworth, Middlesex, England

First published 1995
1 3 5 7 9 10 8 6 4 2

Filmset in 14/15 pt Garamond

Made and printed in Great Britain by Clays Ltd, St Ives plc

A CIP catalogue record for this book is available from the British Library

ISBN 0-525-69035-2

Contents

Bad Girl Warning

This book may be
BAD FOR YOU.
This book is a
BAD GIRL BOOK.
This book is about
MARMALADE ATKINS,
thought by many to be the
WORST GIRL IN THE WORLD.
Marmalade Atkins thinks bad thoughts and does
bad things and puts herself about. What is worse,
she gets away with it. This is a very regrettable
state of affairs, but the truth must be told. If you
don't like books about bad girls –
STOP READING NOW.

So you *like* stories about bad girls who put themselves about? All right. No accounting for tastes. But before we go any further, you should read this
BAD DONKEY WARNING.
You may have seen sweet-looking donkeys harmlessly munching grass or gazing wistfully over fences. You may even have had donkey rides on the beach and lived to tell the tale. Rufus is not that sort of donkey. Rufus has strong views about donkey rides. He says he thinks it's about time donkeys got to ride on people, instead of the other way round. He *looks* very sweet, and he *can* be very gentle, but don't bank on it. He might decide to nuzzle you gently and accept your proffered carrot, but if he doesn't like the look of you, he's just as likely to push you over and stand on you. He's rude. He's sarcastic. He hurts people's feelings, chews their buttons and kicks their cars to bits.

Apart from that, he's all right.

BAD SPORTS WARNING
There are some very bad sports in this book, and ... no, I think that's enough warnings. Let's get on with the gruesome details, shall we?

Back to Basics

The Worst Girl in the World was feeling a bit fed up, and so would you be in her situation. She was in a small field surrounded by a tall electric fence, which was switched on, and big iron gates, which were locked. In the corner of the field there was a stable, open on one side, in which she could shelter if it rained. There were no books, no toys, no television, no Game Boy, no Walkperson. Her only companion was a scruffy old ginger donkey called Rufus, who looked as fed up as Marmalade felt. Marmalade Atkins was a prisoner.

And who were the villains responsible for this cruel treatment? I am sorry to say that their names were Mr and Mrs Atkins, and they were Marmalade's very own parents. There were some mitigating circumstances: Marmalade *had* blown up the washing machine while carrying out a small electrical experiment, and she *had* put purple dye into her mother's shampoo bottle. The effects of the latter had caused Mr Atkins so much amusement that he had fallen off the kitchen stool and broken his ankle. Mrs Atkins, however, was not at all pleased, and as soon as her husband was able to hobble about, she insisted on something being done about Marmalade.

If any of you happen to be parents of Bad Girls and on the look-out for new wheezes for dealing with your wicked offspring, don't be tempted to imitate Mr and Mrs Atkins. Imprisoning your children is probably against some silly law or other, and you have no idea how expensive electric fences are these days. It was convenient for Mr and Mrs Atkins that they lived in a pretty farmhouse in the depths of the countryside, with plenty of spare fields just waiting to be turned into Open Air Prisons for Little Girls, but most parents of Bad Girls aren't so lucky.

The fact is, Marmalade's mother and father were pretty bad characters themselves. Mr Atkins called himself a Small Businessman, but Fat Crook would be a more accurate description. He wasn't the sort of crook who robs banks, more the sort who tries to sell Buckingham Palace or Madame Tussaud's to unsuspecting foreign tourists. He was obliged to sell a lot of things that didn't really belong to him for large sums of money, because Mrs Atkins was an absolute whizz at getting on the phone to Harrods and ordering vast quantities of expensive things like caviare and diamonds. (Or electric fences, come to that. You can get anything from Harrods if you're prepared to pay for it.)

'It'll be *so* good for her!' Mrs Atkins enthused,

polishing off the last chocolate in a particularly delicious box from Fortnum and Mason's. 'Fresh air, you know! Exercise! Nature, and so on! No nasty books and comics and videos – just simple country life!'

'You don't think she might turn into a little savage, sort of thing?' said Mr Atkins doubtfully. (Actually, he didn't particularly care what Marmalade turned into, so long as she was on one side of an electric fence and he was on the other, but he liked to sound as if he did.)

'*Turn* into a little savage?' shrieked his wife, banging him on the knee with her gold bracelet. 'She *is* a little savage! Always has been! *I* don't know what we've done to deserve her!'

'Well, our little girl is safe and sound now, Muriel,' said Mr Atkins. 'And I feel a whole lot better with that ginger donkey behind bars too – I've never liked the way he looks at me. I feel relaxed enough to have a large brandy and forty winks.'

Inside three minutes he was happily snoring away on the sofa while Mrs Atkins broke open another box of chocs and got on the blower to Harrods.

Mr and Mrs Atkins were happier than they had been for ages, but out in the field it was damp and chilly, and Marmalade Atkins was getting more fed up than ever. She glared at Rufus, who was peacefully munching some juicy tufts of damp grass.

'Look here, Rufus, this is no good,' she said. 'Why don't we escape or something?'

Rufus looked up and blinked his sleepy old eyes. Then he gave a very loud and sarcastic sounding 'Hee-*haw*!', pulled up another great tuft of grass and chomped on it noisily.

'Yes, I know. It's all very well for you,' said Marmalade. 'You've got your thick coat on. You *like* eating grass. I realise that. But what about me? I mean, whose side are you on, Rufus? Whose donkey are you supposed to be? Mine!'

Rufus looked up again, not quite so sleepily. In fact there was rather a mean look in his yellow eyes, and Marmalade knew why. Rufus didn't belong to anyone in his opinion, and as for sides, he was on his own side.

'But what about the principle of the thing?' continued Marmalade, taking another tack. 'They've made you a prisoner, Rufus. They've locked you up. I thought you were a Wild Free Spirit! What happened to the Ass They Couldn't Tame? I've known you to tunnel out of tighter spots than this. Can this be the same donkey that led the Great Escape from Warwick Race-course? Is this the Rufus who wrecked the Horse of the Year Show?'

Apparently not.

Rufus took no notice of Marmalade, but carried on tearing up the thick juicy tufts of grass and munching them while the pale afternoon sun glinted on his rough, stubbly ginger coat, with its sandy bits and rosy bits and dark brown bits.

'Rufus! Have you gone ordinary on me, or what?'

No answer. It looked as if he had.

'Right,' said Marmalade. 'S'pose we'll have to play football again then.'

Marmalade's football had been won by her father at a fund-raising dinner. It was third prize in a raffle, and bore the autographs of all the England football team. Unfortunately, they weren't very good at the time this story takes place, so the ball wasn't worth much. (In fact, second prize in the raffle had been a football *without* any autographs.) But Marmalade's ball was perfectly OK for playing with, and she played every day.

Marmalade had got quite good at football, and so had Rufus. He would stand up against one wall of the stable, which was the goal. Then she would take the ball down to the end of the field and advance on the goal in a great swerving run, darting round imaginary defenders and muttering and growling to herself, before letting fly at the goal as hard as she could. After she had hit Rufus once or twice with the ball, he started to take an interest and developed a remarkable goalkeeping technique, intercepting shots from every angle using all four hooves and occasionally his broad bottom.

That was what they were doing when the little black van came down the bumpy track from the main road. Not many people came to visit the Atkinses, except delivery vans from Harrods and Fortnum and Mason's, and this didn't look like a delivery van. It had a neat little sign on it with a picture of a fierce-looking bird and the words HAWKEYE HOOKYWATCH LTD. Marmalade and Rufus wandered over to the fence as the man in the van wound down the window. He looked a bit like a hawk himself – small and spiky, with a great big beaky nose, black shiny hair combed straight back, and sharp glittering eyes. His name, in case you're wondering, was Harry Hawk, and he was a sort of bounty-hunter, catching truants for reward – bad girls a speciality, no girl too big or too small. He was in fact the most famous and feared truant-taker in the land, but Marmalade didn't know that yet.

'Morning, cock!' said Marmalade. 'What can we do for you?'

'Little girl, let me ask you one simple question,' said Harry Hawk. '*Shouldn't you be in school?*'

'Let me ask *you* one simple question,' said Marmalade. 'Is that your nose or are you training to be a parrot?'

Harry Hawk grinned. 'I like a girl with a sense of humour,' he said. 'I like to share a joke with a little girl, I do, I do. But generally I tend to have the last laugh, I must confess.'

He seemed very amused by this remark; in fact he laughed so much that his van shook and rattled.

'Catch you later, little girl,' he said, and he wound up the window, drove up to the farmhouse, parked his little black van next to Mr Atkins's Rolls-Royce, and rang the bell.

'But you don't understand,' said Mr Atkins. 'We're just locking her up for our own protection!'

'Think of her as a sort of piranha in jeans, Mr Hawk,' said Mrs Atkins helpfully.

'Ought to be in school, though,' said Harry Hawk. 'Can't have girls playing hooky.'

'We'd *like* her to go to school, honest, squire,' said Mr Atkins.

'In the Galapagos Islands for preference,' said Mrs Atkins, with a rather hysterical laugh.

'But the schools won't have her, you see, squire. We've tried her everywhere from Cringe Hall to Eton – expelled every time. Even the nuns chucked her out in the end. She's been bunged out of more schools than I've had hot dinners. It's hopeless – hopeless, Mr Hawk, sir.'

'Mr Atkins, I've got news for you,' said Harry Hawk. 'Schools are changing. Opting out. Privatising. Putting things on a business footing.

7

There's money in kids these days, even bad ones.'

'Really?' said Mr Atkins, sitting up. 'Have a cigar, squire.'

'The school I recommend for your little girl, Mr and Mrs Atkins, is Hard Tack Hall,' said Harry Hawk, putting Mr Atkins's cigar in his top pocket for later. (Harry Hawk didn't like cigars much, but had never been known to refuse a free offer. As a matter of fact, he was going to like this particular cigar even less than usual, because it happened to be an exploding one that Marmalade had slipped into her dad's cigar box before her imprisonment, and when Harry Hawk lit it up on his way home, he nearly blew the roof off his van.)

'Hard Tack Hall?' said Mrs Atkins doubtfully. 'Is it frightfully expensive? We are of course disgustingly rich, but we prefer to spend our money on jewellery and chocs and so forth rather than our little girl.'

'Very wise,' said Harry Hawk, 'and you will be pleased to hear that apart from the introduction fee, Hard Tack Hall is free of charge.'

'Jolly good,' said Mr Atkins. 'Who do we pay the introduction fee to? Your good self, I imagine?'

Harry Hawk nodded, and fifty pounds in cash changed hands.

'You won't regret it, Mr and Mrs Atkins,' said Harry Hawk. 'Hard Tack Hall is a Back to

Basics school. They'll soon sort your little girl out.'

Harry Hawk drove his little black van back to Marmalade's Open Air Prison, and Mr Atkins unlocked the gate.

'That looks a nice little donkey,' said Harry Hawk. 'Ever thought of selling him?'

'Fifty quid to you, sir,' said Mr Atkins.

'Hey!' said Marmalade. 'He's not yours to sell!'

'Take no notice of her, Mr Hawk,' said Marmalade's father. 'She's under age.'

'How would you like to be my personal donkey, little feller?' said Harry Hawk to Rufus. Rufus looked at Harry Hawk thoughtfully, then stood on his foot, ate two buttons off his jacket, and kicked a big dent in the back of his shiny black van.

'I've changed me mind,' said Harry Hawk. 'And I'll have another fifty for the dent in the van.'

Hard Tack Hall had been a perfectly ordinary school until Mr Suckling-Pygge had taken over as headmaster and started making changes. Mr Suckling-Pygge was a great believer in Discipline and Hard Sums and Multiplication Tables and Old-Fashioned Ways in General. He had read a lot of stories about what schools were like in the old days, when all the teachers were very fierce and all the children were very meek and mild, and he thought that was just the sort of school he would like to be in charge of, and he was just the sort of man to be in charge of it.

Mr Sucking-Pygge was always very pleased with himself, and when he had nothing better to do he liked to admire himself in mirrors, smirking and pouting in various appealing poses, sometimes holding a cane, sometimes a mortarboard. Nobody else thought he was a very pretty sight. He had a round piggy face with little round piggy eyes, and his head looked like a size too large for his narrow little body in its snugly fitting double-breasted suit. In fact, he looked remarkably like a pig in a suit, but as nobody had ever dared to tell him that, he was not aware of it. He thought he looked very nice indeed.

When he looked at Marmalade standing on the carpet in front of his desk on her first day, he didn't like the look of her at all. 'Marmalade Atkins,' he said, 'at Hard Tack Hall we believe in Victorian values, and you look *dangerously modern* to me.'

'What's Victorian values then, cock?' said Marmalade.

Mr Suckling Pygge was so taken aback that his voice went all squeaky.

'Victorian values are about working hard and playing hard and having respect for your elders and betters, and you are a very naughty, disrespectful little girl!'

'I know that,' said Marmalade. 'I'm famous for it. But do you know you look like a pig in a suit?'

No one had ever been quite as rude as that to Mr Suckling-Pygge, even though he had met and tamed a good many Difficult Girls in his time. He didn't mind Difficult Girls, and the government paid him double the usual fee for each one he tamed, but Marmalade was worse than a Difficult Girl – she was more of a Diabolical Girl, and Mr Suckling-Pygge made a resolution to ask for four times the usual fee in her case.

'Uniform first,' he said. 'Pigtails and pinafores for girls, blazers and caps for boys.'

'I haven't got a pigtail,' said Marmalade, 'not being a pig. Can I borrow yours, cock?'

'Oh, you naughty little girl!' squeaked Mr Suckling-Pygge, going bright pink with rage. 'But I'll tame you, make no doubt of that! Monitors! Monitors! Duty Monitors forward!'

He gave a quick toot on the shiny silver whistle that hung round his neck, and four big girls rushed in and grabbed hold of Marmalade by the arms and legs. These were the Duty Monitors. Their names were Monica, Japonica, Veronica and Judy, and they were hard as nails and tough as old boots. Before Marmalade knew what was happening, she was rushed into the Assembly Hall and chained by the neck and the ankle to an old-fashioned desk in the very front

row. It had a hard old wooden seat and nasty old black iron legs. In a top corner was a little china inkwell full of smelly old blue-black ink. The seat had been worn smooth and shiny by the bottoms of a million unhappy girls, and the lid was covered over and over with their scratched initials, and warped and blistered by the salt flow of their despairing tears.

The clamps and shackles made it difficult to move, but by scrunching her neck and swivelling her eyeballs Marmalade was able to see that there were fifty rows of desks on the Girls' side of the hall, with the Worst Girls at the front and the Best Girls at the back. The Worst Girls of all, of whom Marmalade was one, had little blackboards hung round their necks with I AM BAD in curly writing on them; and the Best Girls had I AM GOOD embroidered on their pinafores. On the other side of the hall were fifty rows of Good and Bad Boys, also chained to their desks.

Mr Suckling-Pygge strutted to the front of the hall, swishing his cane and flapping his own gown about. 'Boys and Girls of Hard Tack Hall!' he squeaked. 'Get on with your Hard Sums! Work and Misery in the mornings, Art and Recreation in the afternoons; that's what Victorian values are all about!'

There were a few moans, a few groans, and a few sighs, but nobody protested. Nobody shouted out cheeky remarks or threw inkwells about. Marmalade tested out the strength of her shackles. They were very strong. They were also very tight, too tight even for a skinny-wristed girl like her to wriggle out of them. She tried rocking her desk, but it was bolted to the floor. There was nothing to stop her making witty remarks, but if she did Mr Suckling-Pygge would probably get his monitors to torture her, and she had already had enough of that.

Marmalade decided that the best thing to do was to play it crafty, and do the Hard Sums.

It might surprise you to know that Marmalade wasn't at all bad at Hard Sums. She had had to help her father fiddle his income tax more than once, and Rufus had shown her how to calculate the odds when betting on likely-looking young horses. She picked up a squeaky old pen, dipped it into the dark and smelly old inkwell and, resisting the temptation to flick a few inkblots in the direction of Mr Suckling-Pygge's shiny pink snout, she got down to work.

By the end of the morning Marmalade had finished forty-three Hard Sums, most of them Long Division (thought by many to be the hardest sums of all). Mr Suckling-Pygge was extremely surprised, and very pleased.

'Well, little girl,' he said, beaming his special smile at her. (He thought his special smile made him look stern but kind, and had no idea it made him look like someone who has just eaten a slug by mistake instead of a sausage.) 'It looks as if a Certain Little Girl has decided to Shape Up and Toe the Line.'

'You're right, cock – I mean, sir,' said Marmalade humbly. 'I used to think I was dead hard, but now I realise I have met my match in you, sir. It's Marmalade the Good Girl from now on.'

'Excellent! Excellent!' said Mr Suckling-Pygge. 'Another success story for Hard Tack Hall! You may have three hard biscuits and a nice glass of water for lunch!'

After lunch it was time for Art and Recreation.

'Form two lines, please!' squeaked Mr Suckling-Pygge. 'Football for the boys and Embroidery for the girls!'

All the girls and boys got into their lines, the boys with their smart little football boots and the girls with their samplers and pincushions.

'Here, hang on, cock – I mean, sir – I mean, dear, clever, kind Mr Suckling-Pygge,' said Marmalade. 'Can't I have a go at the footy instead of the embroidery?'

'Certainly not!' said Mr Suckling-Pygge. 'Girls do not play footy at Hard Tack Hall! They do embroidery and learn to be young ladies!'

'That's sexual discrimination,' said Marmalade.

'Indeed it is!' beamed Mr Suckling-Pygge. 'Boys! Here is a strange little girl! She says she wants to play *footy*!'

All the boys of Hard Tack Hall fell about chortling in a manly way.

'Cripes! I say! What a corker! Whoever heard of girls playing *footy*? Shall we help you chain her to the desk, sir?'

'No,' said Mr Suckling-Pygge. 'I don't think that will be necessary. Off you go to the football field, boys! Get on with your embroidery, girls!'

'Please, Mr Suckling-Pygge,' said Marmalade in a shy and wheedling tone.

'Yes, my dear? What is it?'

'Can I sit at your feet to do my embroidery, gazing up at you from time to time in admiration? I have read in a book that girls did this in olden times.'

Mr Suckling-Pygge thought it over. It was an unusual request, but a very charming one. He would be able to tell the chaps at the Rotary Club about it – how Back to Basics had reformed the Worst Girl in the World.

'Why, yes, you may, Marmalade,' said Mr Suckling-Pygge.

So Marmalade sat at Mr Suckling-Pygge's feet all afternoon, gazing up at him from time to time in admiration while she embroidered the seat of his trousers to the piano stool. Mr Suckling-Pygge was so busy looking at himself in the mirror and wondering whether or not to part his hair in the middle that he didn't notice what was happening until it was too late.

'Finished, sir!' said Marmalade.

Mr Suckling-Pygge stood up, feeling uneasy. Something was wrong, but he didn't know what. His trousers felt strangely weighty, as if someone were pulling them from behind.

'Finished?' he said. 'But where is your embroidery?'

'It's behind you, sir,' said Marmalade shyly.

Mr Suckling-Pygge turned round, and was shocked to hear the unfamiliar sound of laughter. The girls of Hard Tack Hall were laughing at their headmaster! It was hard for them not to, because the piano stool was hanging from the seat of his trousers like a huge, lumpy, wooden tail.

He felt behind him cautiously, and pulled. Nothing happened. Marmalade had really stitched him up tight.

'Monitors! Get this thing off me at once!'

Monica, Veronica, Japonica and Judy leapt on to the stage. Monica and Veronica took hold of Mr Suckling-Pygge and Japonica and Judy took hold of the piano stool and pulled. They were very strong girls. The piano stool tore free, but so did the seat of Mr Suckling-Pygge's smart suit, revealing a very snazzy pair of red and white striped underpants.

'Like your knickers, cock!' said Marmalade.

Mr Suckling-Pygge turned round. He had gone very red in the face.

'Marmalade Atkins,' he squeaked, 'you are expelled!'

*

The next day, a new boy arrived at Hard Tack Hall. He was rather small and skinny, but very smartly dressed in a tight little double-breasted blazer and a smart little striped cap. Mr Suckling-Pygge liked the look of him very much indeed.

'Well, well, well! You look a smart little chap! What can we do for you?' he said.

'Please, sir, my daddy sent me here because he says Hard Tack Hall is the best school in the world.'

'Your daddy is right,' smirked Mr Suckling-Pygge. 'And what is your name, little chap?'

'Er . . . Marmaduke Watkins.'

'I see.' Mr Suckling-Pygge felt uneasy for a moment – he had some vague memory of something that was not very nice. He wrinkled up his piggy little nose and thought, but nothing came to mind. And anyway, what could be sinister about this sweet little fellow? Still, better make sure he was the right type.

'We run a tight ship here, you know,' he told the new boy. 'Work hard and play hard, no time for slackers!'

'Will there be Hard Sums and footy, sir?'

'Indeed there will, little chap! Indeed there will!'

'Jolly good, sir! Just what I like best!' said Marmalade Atkins.

'Hmmm,' said Mr Suckling-Pygge. He still felt a bit suspicious, but he couldn't think why.

*

The morning passed away quite peacefully. Thanks to her disguise, Marmalade found herself in the Good Boys section, between two very nice little boys called Norman Pratt and Norman Spratt.

'Gosh, Watkins!' gasped Norman Pratt. 'You're fearfully good at Hard Sums, isn't he, Spratty?'

'Gosh, yes, Pratty, I should jolly well say he is!' said Norman Spratt.

'Wait till you see me on the footy field,' said Marmalade.

'Wait till you see *us*! We're ace, aren't we, Spratty?' said Norman Pratt, but he looked a bit anxious.

'Wicked!' said Spratty, but he didn't look too sure about it.

As a matter of fact, Norman Pratt and Norman Spratt were not too brilliant at football. Nothing wrong with that, but Hard Tack Hall was one of those schools where, if you were a boy, you were supposed to be brilliant at football and dead keen on it too, and if you were a girl you were supposed to feel the same way about embroidery. Mad, I know, but a lot of schools are like that.

After the boys and girls had eaten their Hard Tack Hall lunch of dry biscuits and water, all the girls got out their needles and all the boys trooped out to the footy field with Mr Suckling-Pygge, who was wearing a shiny pink tracksuit.

He gave a little toot on his silver whistle, and the boys gathered round him.

'Now, let's see,' said Mr Suckling-Pygge, a teasing smile playing at the corners of his piggy pink lips. 'What shall the teams be today?'

'Sir! Sir! Aces and Weeds, sir!' squeaked all the little boys.

'Very well,' said Mr Suckling-Pygge. 'Aces and Weeds it is! Line up, boys! Aces on the left and Weeds on the right! Marmaduke Watkins, you had better start off in the Weeds with Pratt and Spratt.'

'Come on then, Watters,' said Norman Pratt sadly.

'Here, cock – I mean, Pratty,' said Marmalade. 'I thought you and Spratty were supposed to be ace at footy.'

'Well, um, actually, Watters, we're not all that ace really, are we, Spratty?'

'Not really, no,' said Norman Spratt. 'Afraid we told you a bit of a porky there, Watters. Not really ace at footy at all.'

'Pratty and Spratty? They're weedy at footy!' sneered Gary Snide, the goalkeeper of the Aces team, a big boy with mean eyes and sharp elbows and a horrible evil laugh. 'Hurgle, hurgle, hurgle!' he laughed. 'I'm a poet, and don't I know it! Listen to this, chaps – *Pratty* and *Spratty* are *weedy* at *footy*! All together!'

All the sneaks and toadies joined in because they were frightened of Gary Snide and his mean ways and sharp elbows. 'Pratty and Spratty are weedy at footy! Pratty and Spratty are weedy at footy!'

Norman Pratt went very red and hung his head, and Norman Spratt brushed a tear from his eye.

'All right, chaps!' said Mr Suckling-Pygge with a merry laugh. 'Ragging the Weeds is jolly good fun, but let's get real. I'm in the business of turning boys into men and footy's the name of the game!'

'Hang on a minute, cock – I mean, sir,' said Marmalade. 'Why are all the best players on one side and all the worst on the other?'

'Because football is like life, Watkins,' said Mr Suckling-Pygge. 'Competition! Survival of the fittest! Let battle commence! Play up, play up and play the game!'

He blew the whistle and the game started. It was horrible. The Aces were all big and strong and mean and the Weeds were all small and weak and, well, weedy. Most of them didn't even *like* footy. Some of them had sneaking yearnings to be doing embroidery. Every time the Aces scored, Gary Snide laughed his horrible laugh: 'Hurgle, hurgle, hurgle! Hurgle, hurgle, hurgle!' It sounded like something unspeakable stuck in a waste pipe.

By half-time, the score was seventeen-nil to the Aces. Seventeen hurgle, hurgle, hurgles. All of the Weeds were exhausted and dispirited, some had been trampled into the mud, and Pratty and Spratty were in tears.

And what was Marmaduke Watkins doing all this time? He was leaning against the goalposts with his arms folded, reading the *Beano*. Mr Suckling-Pygge was busy running up and down blowing his whistle and getting pinker and pinker in the face, and it was quite a while before he noticed Marmalade, but when he did he was very shocked.

'Marmaduke Watkins!' he squeaked indignantly. 'Are you a beastly little slacker?'

'I am, sir!' said Marmalade cheerfully.

'But I thought you were supposed to be keen on footy, boy!'

'I know, sir. I know. I just seem to have gone off it all of a sudden. Isn't it amazing, sir?'

'Don't bandy words with me, Marmaduke Watkins! I demand that you enter into the spirit of the game! This minute!'

'All right, then, cock,' said Marmalade. 'If you insist.'

She rolled up her comic and stuck it in the back of her shorts and spat on her hands. (Many great players do that; no one knows why.) The next time the ball came her way, she set off on a great swerving run, muttering and growling to herself. The Weeds were amazed and the Aces were baffled. The Aces were not in fact nearly as brilliant as they thought they were. Their idea of tackling was to charge at the person with the ball and barge him out of the way. They weren't used to skinny-dodging tactics, and Marmalade skinny-dodged her way in and out of them with ease, while they barged into each other and charged into the goalposts. When a particularly big fat Ace called Porpoise Perkins came charging at her, Marmalade slipped aside at the last split second, and he careered on right into Mr Suckling-Pygge, knocking all the breath out of him so that he couldn't blow his whistle. Now Marmalade had only the goalkeeper to beat: Gary Snide, sneering at her between his goalposts.

'Come on, weedy Watkins! Let's see what you can do. Nothing gets past Gary Snide!' She steadied herself, took aim, and let fly, just as she had done so many times with Rufus in her Open Air Prison.

She gave Gary Snide her special favourite bendy-banana shot. It skidded off the side of her boot and whistled through the air like a greased cannonball. It veered to the left, veered to the right, and then straightened up at the last minute. Gary Snide tried to jump in both directions at once, and he had his arms spread wide when the ball hit him in the midriff, so hard that he shot backwards into the netting, where he lay tangled up and gasping for breath like a stranded shark.

'Haven't you forgotten something, cock?' said Marmalade. Gary Snide stared at her, still gasping and struggling with the netting.

'Hurgle, hurgle, hurgle!' said Marmalade Atkins as all the Weeds came running up to pat her on the back.

'Great shot, Watters!' said Norman Pratt.

'Brilliant footers, Watters!' said Norman Spratt.

Mr Suckling-Pygge was still lying panting on the halfway line under the unconscious body of Porpoise Perkins. He was wondering whether reffing footy was really his thing after all. Perhaps, as headmaster, he should stick to quieter pursuits. He could always wear his shiny pink tracksuit to wine and cheese parties, or just loll about the lounge in it, watching his favourite programmes on telly. That would be *much* nicer than lying about in the mud with a lot of silly little boys. He was just beginning to wish very fervently that it was all over and he was lying in a nice hot bath, when he saw that strange little new boy Marmaduke Watkins leaning over him.

'Home time, sir. I'll just give your whistle a little toot, all right?' But Mr Suckling-Pygge was too weak to answer.

Marmalade gave a long blast on the whistle.

'Right, chaps. Footy's over for today. Three cheers for the jolly old referee!'

'Hurrah! Hurrah! Hurrah!' cheered the boys of Hard Tack Hall.

'That was a jolly good footy match; well, the end bit was anyway,' said Norman Pratt, as they watched Gary Snide, Porpoise Perkins and Mr Suckling-Pygge being loaded into ambulances.

'Certainly was, Spratty! And now for a jolly good shower!' said Norman Spratt. 'You coming, Watters?'

'Er . . . better not,' said Marmalade Atkins.

Football is Not About Goals

'So, how are you getting on at school then, Marmalade?' said Mr Atkins. He was in a particularly good mood that evening, having just got back from a trip to Derbyshire, where he had sold a stately home called Chatsworth House to a bunch of unsuspecting foreign tourists for fifty thousand pounds. (This would have been a bargain for the tourists if the stately home had been Mr Atkins's to sell, but of course it wasn't.)

'All right,' said Marmalade cautiously. She didn't think much of Hard Tack Hall, but if she complained about it or said she enjoyed it too much, her parents might take her away and put her somewhere even worse.

'*I* am not impressed with the establishment,' said Mrs Atkins. 'They seem to think she is a *boy*!'

'Well, maybe she is,' said Marmalade's dad. 'These teachers know a lot, you know. She looks like a boy to me. Tie, trousers – yes, that's a boy in my book. Maybe she's changed into a boy. Have you changed into a boy, Marmalade?'

'Yes, Dad, I have,' said Marmalade. 'My name is Marmaduke Watkins now.'

'There you are then,' said Mr Atkins. 'Wonders never cease, eh?'

'Oh, shut up, Atkins, you clodhopping imbecile!' shrieked his wife, slapping him several times across the face with a side of smoked salmon which had just arrived from Fortnum and Mason's. 'This will just be some new way of Mucking About she's discovered to drive her poor mother potty! It's going to take a lot of caviare and champagne to get me over this!'

'Maybe she's having an identity crisis,' said Mr Atkins. 'I've heard of them, you know. It's when you forget who you are, sort of thing, and take on a different personality altogether. People have committed terrible crimes in an identity crisis, and it's not their fault at all, because they thought they were someone entirely different at the time. Here, that's an idea! I could try that if I get in trouble over that stately home business. I could say I was having an identity crisis and I thought I was the Duke of Derbyshire. "Here's my friend Lord Marmaduke Watkins," I shall say. "He's as barmy as I am and he'll back me up to the very hilt!"'

Mrs Atkins waggled the side of smoked salmon in a threatening way, and her husband subsided.

'Just my little joke, Muriel. You have to have a laugh now and then, don't you? What d'you reckon, Lord Watkins?'

'I'm not barmy, Dad. I'm just Mucking About – honest!'

'Aha!' shrieked Mrs Atkins. 'She admits it!

Mucking About! Trying to drive her poor mother to distraction!'

'I'm not – honest, Mum!' said Marmalade. 'I just Muck About because it's what I do. It's my job to Muck About, see, and it's your job and the teachers' job to try and stop me. That's how I see it. And if everybody just got on with their jobs and stopped moaning and complaining the world would be a better place, that's what I think. It's not my fault, is it? I'm doing my job, after all.'

'Well, you can't say fairer than that, can you, Muriel?' said Mr Atkins, who had been quite impressed by Marmalade's line of reasoning. 'Who says that young people today aren't pulling their weight? Here's our Marmalade putting all her little heart and soul into her Mucking About, and what support does she get? I call it a scandal and a crying shame.'

'Atkins,' said his wife.

'Yes, my dear?'

'If I hear another word from you or your daughter this evening I shall have one of my attacks.'

Marmalade and her father looked at each other and put their hands over their mouths. When people talk about having attacks, they usually just mean that they get upset or come over all faint. When Marmalade's mother had an attack, it meant that she attacked other people, often with blunt instruments, and these other people often had to go to hospital as a result. I know, I know – this isn't the way to treat your nearest and dearest, but the Atkins family was a *problem family*, all right?

Mrs Atkins reached for the Harrods catalogue and picked up the telephone, and Marmalade and her father crept out of the room. Mr Atkins put on his tweed hat and went down to the sty to talk to Rover the Free-range Piglet, which always calmed him down. It didn't do a lot for Rover the Free-range Piglet, though. He hated people poking him with sticks and going 'Arrr'. He was planning to be a bit of a problem pig when he was old enough.

Marmalade mooched down to the field to see Rufus, who had spent a pleasant and uneventful day doing ordinary donkey things. He had made a new hole in the hedge and shown the cows on the next farm how to get through it. He had had a long roll in some mud, which had left him looking even more scruffy and decrepit than usual. He had been to see his young girlfriend Jenny, who liked her boyfriends to look scruffy and decrepit, and given her a few lessons in how to do the Hee-haw Zig-zag.

The Hee-haw Zig-zag was Rufus's speciality. It consisted of charging up behind people (or, preferably, horses; or, best of all, horses with people riding on their backs) and hee-hawing loudly and continuously while galloping in a series of zig-zags. The horses hated this and

29

would jump about in a panicky way, throwing their riders into cowpats and nettle clumps. When Rufus and Jenny had practised long enough, they went down the lane to the Lurnatrot Riding School and practised Hee-haw Zigzags on the Pony Club. All the ponies went ape and threw their little riders into cowpats and nettle clumps. Then Rufus went back to his stable for a kip, feeling quite satisfied with his day.

And that was where Marmalade found him, blinking his bleary old eyes and chewing reflectively on a pair of old jodhpurs.

'Hello, Rufus, old cock!' she said, not expecting any answer. 'What's going on?'

'Not a lot, Marmalade Atkins,' said a creaky old voice. 'What's going on with you?' Rufus was talking again!

'Rufus!' she said. 'I thought you'd gone back to being normal.'

'Harrumph!' said Rufus dismissively.

'Well, why haven't you been talking to me?'

'Didn't have nothing to say, did I?'

'Well, you might have let me know. I thought you'd given it up altogether. Does this mean you're going to start putting yourself about again?'

'Might do,' said Rufus. 'Might come down that school of yours, one of these days, put meself about a bit there.'

'Yeah,' said Marmalade. 'Why not?'

She rested her head against his shaggy old

shoulder. Rufus felt warm and dirty, and smelt very richly of himself. She felt happy. Mucking About and getting up people's noses was all right, a good job as jobs went, but it was nice to have a rest now and then.

Not many miles away, a short, bald-headed man in a red, white and blue tracksuit was pounding across the countryside, muttering furiously to himself. 'Come on, Ron!' he cried as his short fat legs twinkled over the dewy turf. 'Gimme hundred per cent! Go for it! Work that body! Push, push, push! That's it, Ron! Good boy! Hundred and ten per cent! Hundred and *twenty*! Good *boy*, Ron! Go, go, *go*!' He wobbled. He stumbled. He fell down. He got up. He sweated. He panted. He gasped and he groaned. But on he went, on and on and on.

The name of this man was Ron Drayne, and he *was* having an identity crisis. Ron Drayne was the manager of the English football team, and (as you will remember) England were not doing very well. In fact, they had lost their last seventeen games, and Ron Drayne was just about the most unpopular man in the whole country, after the Prime Minister. People yelled and jeered and shook their fists at him in the street. People even bought 'Ron Drayne' squeaky toys and gave them to their dogs to towzer and chew up. Everywhere he went he would hear people chanting songs about him, such as:

Ron Drayne,
He's a pain.
Chuck him in the toilet.
Flush him down the drain.

This sort of thing can get to a sensitive man, and Ron Drayne was a very sensitive man. He had tried his best. He had given his all. A hundred per cent. More than a hundred per cent. He had trained all day and all night, and still his team didn't win. And now the strain had got to him. Suddenly, in the middle of a press conference, with everyone asking him rude questions like when was he going to resign, and why was he such a turnip, something had snapped inside him. He had stumbled out of the conference, past the photographers with their whizzing motor drives and their blinding flashes, and run all the way to Warwickshire. He had had a close escape near Oxford, when some enraged football fans had recognised him and chased him across the fields as far as Banbury, but he managed to shake them off. In Banbury he pulled the hood of his tracksuit up over his face and bought a false moustache and glasses in a joke shop, before ploughing on over the field and hills, with no idea where he was going.

Ron Drayne was near total exhaustion and almost at the end of his tether, when he saw a pretty little farm ahead of him, and he stumbled up the slope towards a small stable at the corner of the field. He was vaguely aware of a dark, shaggy presence in the stable – something warm, something with a steady, slow, slightly wheezy breath – but he was far too exhausted to do anything about it. He sank gratefully into the straw and fell into a deep sleep.

When he woke up it was morning, and there, staring down at him, were a scruffy old ginger donkey and a ferocious-looking little girl.

'Morning, cock!' said Marmalade.

'Never mind morning, cock,' said Rufus. 'This is my stable and my straw, mister. You take liberties with me and I'll take liberties with you. I got a good mind to chew all your buttons off, I have.'

Ron Drayne started to tremble. 'Am I dreaming?' he said. 'Or have I died and gone to heaven?'

'Neither, cock,' said Marmalade. 'This is Warwickshire. My name's Marmalade Atkins and this is my donkey Rufus.'

'Not her donkey,' said Rufus. 'I'm me own donkey, I am. I was on this farm before she was ever heard of, or her dad either.'

Ron Drayne blinked. 'Look,' he said, 'is that donkey talking or are you a ventriloquist?' Something was tickling his nose. Oh, yes. It was that false moustache. He reached up and took it off, and his glasses came off too, as they were all in one piece.

'Here!' said Marmalade. 'I know you. You're that Ron Drayne, aren't you? My dad's got a photo of you he throws darts at sometimes.'

Ron Drayne groaned. Was there to be no escape from shame and ridicule?

'Never mind, cock,' said Marmalade. 'Your secret is safe with us. You can hide out here for a bit if you like. Rufus'll look after you. He's a brilliant minder. Dead strict, though. He used to mind racehorses.'

'That was in the old days,' said Rufus rather mournfully. 'Them was the days!'

'Too right, mate,' said Ron Drayne, who was getting quite used to the idea of talking to a donkey. 'People had a bit of respect in them days.'

'Well, this is it, mate,' said Rufus, who was beginning to warm to Ron Drayne.

'What is this? The Who Can Be Most Boring competition?' said Marmalade rather rudely. 'Listen, I can't hang about, I've got to go to school in a minute. Shall I nip into the kitchen and nick you something to eat before I go, or will you be all right sharing a bit of hay and stuff with Rufus?'

'Could I have a meat pie, please?' said Ron Drayne humbly.

'Don't think we've got any,' said Marmalade. 'D'you think you could manage with a smoked salmon sandwich or two and a bottle of bubbly? I think that's all Mum usually keeps in the fridge.'

'Yeah, all right, ta very much. Ron Drayne's not one to make a fuss,' said the England manager generously.

Marmalade went back to the house. She could hear her mother and father still snoring in their beds upstairs. There were a few pots of caviare in the fridge as well as the smoked salmon and bubbly, so she took them down to the stable, where Ron and Rufus were already engaged in a lovely boring conversation about the Old Days.

All right for them! Marmalade had to deal with the present. She had to deal with Modern Times. She had to deal with Hard Tack Hall.

When Marmalade got to school, all the boys and girls were trooping into the Assembly Hall. She took her place on the boys' side, remembering at the last moment that she was supposed to be Marmaduke Watkins. Unfortunately, she had forgotten to dress as a boy.

Mr Suckling-Pygge, who had discharged himself from hospital that morning, was still feeling a little shaky and not quite himself, but here was something that had to be dealt with. He put his spectacles on his little piggy nose and peered at Marmalade, and Marmalade peered back.

'Do I see a little *girl* on the *boys'* side of the hall?' squeaked Mr Suckling-Pygge, in a horrified tone. All the good little boys and girls giggled and tittered. 'What is your name, little girl?'

'Please, sir, Marmaduke Watkins. You remember me, sir? And I'm not a girl, sir, I'm a boy!'

'Then why are you wearing girl's clothing, Watkins?'

'Just for a bit of a jape and a wheeze, sir. Boys will be boys, you know! You like a joke yourself, don't you, sir?'

Now it was Mr Suckling-Pygge's turn to think. Did he like a joke? Should headmasters like jokes? Were jokes on the National Curriculum? He couldn't remember. Perhaps he was having an identity crisis. Better play it safe.

'All right, Watkins. Ha-ha! Very amusing, but there's more important things in life than jokes and japes, you know,' he said. 'Which brings me to footy!'

'Footy, footy, footy! Rah! Rah! Rah!' went all the Hard Tack boys.

'All right. Simmer down, chaps. Now, we have a bit of a crisis on our hands. Next Saturday is the cup-tie against Snobbe Towers. Owing to my injuries sustained on the field yesterday, I shall be unable personally to take charge of the School Team. I hope to appoint a new Games Master in the very near future. And we are also looking for a new goalkeeper. Sadly, Gary Snide has decided to give up football for ever. We all wish him the best of luck with his embroidery.'

'Please, sir,' said Norman Pratt, 'I thought you said embroidery was just for girls.'

'And so it is, except for Gary Snide,' said Mr

Suckling-Pygge irritably. 'Do try not to be a time-waster, Pratt.'

'Please, sir, may Spratty and me do embroidery as well? We think we'd like it better than footy. We're weedy at footy, sir. Everyone knows that. So could we do embroidery, sir, like Gary Snide?'

'Certainly not! What would Hard Tack Hall be like if everybody could do the things they wanted to do?'

'A very nice school, sir?' suggested Marmalade.

'Yes, yes, possibly, but that is not the point!' said Mr Suckling-Pygge irritably, feeling that he was in danger of losing his grip on the situation completely. 'Hard Tack Hall is not in the *business* of being a very nice school!'

'Please, sir, why not, sir?' asked Norman Pratt.

'Yes, sir, why not, sir, please, sir?' asked Norman Spratt.

'Because . . . because . . . because . . .' said Mr Suckling-Pygge, trying desperately to remember . . . 'Because it's in the business of Back to Basics!'

'Look, cock – I mean, please, sir,' said Marmalade, 'could you just explain what all this Back to Basics really is?'

Have you ever had a moment when your mind goes completely blank? It can often happen in school when the teacher asks you a question –

you think you know the answer and you open your mouth, but nothing comes out. Well, it can happen the other way round as well; it can happen to teachers too. Even head-teachers. Mr Suckling-Pygge opened his mouth, but nothing came out. Suddenly he had no idea what Back to Basics was all about. He was just about to go into a fit of the screaming abdabs, when he remembered his Teaching Tactics.

'Let us see who can supply the answer to little Marmaduke's question,' he said. 'Hands up!'

All the big girls in the back row put their hands up.

'Hard Sums, Mr Suckling-Pygge,' said Monica.

'Embroidery for girls and footy for boys, sir,' said Japonica.

'Old-fashioned uniforms and old-fashioned courtesy, sir,' said Veronica.

'And torturing Bad Girls to make them good,' said Judy, with an evil grin.

'Very good! Very good!' said Mr Suckling-Pygge. 'So let's all pull our trousers up, shall we? Those of us who wear them, that is. And that should include you, Marmaduke Watkins! I realise that boys may want to wear frocks from time to time, but I am putting my foot down about this because it could all get far too confusing! I know I like to wear a shiny pink tracksuit but that is neither here nor there. In fact, it is in the wash at the moment because it got all muddy when Perkins fell on me and squashed me flat. That is not funny, Norman Spratt! And another rule is going to be no giggling when I am making one of my great speeches!'

But it was no good. Everyone was laughing now, even the prefects. They hadn't had such a good time at Hard Tack Hall since the school opened.

'Stop it! Stop it! Stop it!' squeaked Mr Suckling-Pygge, hopping from foot to foot in his agitation. 'This is quite considerably and in no small measure not a laughing matter!'

Everyone was laughing now, boys and girls, big and small, goodies and baddies. They wouldn't have been able to stop laughing if they had tried, and nobody was trying. Monica, Japonica, Veronica and Judy were helpless in each other's arms. Pratty and Spratty were rolling on the floor.

Mr Suckling-Pygge hopped up and down so violently that his braces came loose. He was vaguely aware that something was amiss, something else besides the collapse of discipline at Hard Tack Hall, but he didn't know what it was. But the laughter was beginning to subside at last. Gradually the boys and girls of Hard Tack Hall fell silent and watched with open mouths as Mr Suckling-Pygge's smart pin-striped trousers slipped down until they were a crumpled heap around his ankles.

Mr Suckling-Pygge and the boys and girls of Hard Tack Hall stared at each other for a long moment of silence. Funny! thought Mr Suckling-Pygge. There seemed to be a draught coming from somewhere. Unless . . . he looked down. For the second time that week, his underpants were on display. His Union Jack ones this time.

'Like those knickers even better than the last ones, cock!' said Marmalade. 'Smart *and* patriotic.'

Mr Suckling-Pygge started to cry.

'Don't take on, cock!' said Marmalade sympathetically. 'You're just a bit overwrought. Off you go to your room. Eat sweets, read your comic, take it easy for once. We'll sort out your problems for you, don't you worry.'

'Will you really, Marmaduke?' said Mr Suckling-Pygge, smiling through his tears.

'Course we will, cock,' said Marmalade.

Monica, Veronica, Japonica and Judy helped Mr Suckling-Pygge pull up his trousers and led him away to his study.

'Right!' said Marmalade. 'The rest of you can do what you like, but I'm going home.'

When Marmalade got back to the farm, Rufus was standing in the middle of his field staring into space, and Ron Drayne was running very fast in big circles round the edge of the field.

'What's he up to, Rufus?' said Marmalade.

'Don't ask me, Marmalade Atkins. He's barmy, that's what I reckons.'

Ron Drayne staggered to a stop. 'Forty-three circuits,' he said. 'Not enough.'

'It sounds too much to me,' said Marmalade.

'You don't understand,' said Ron Drayne. 'I'm the England manager! Fitness is supremely important! Work that body! Go, go, go!'

'Hang on, cock,' said Marmalade. 'Shouldn't it be the *players* who are fit? What do they do while you're working your body to a frazzle?'

Ron Drayne scratched his head. 'Dunno, really. I think they go clubbing, and drink beer and that. And, you know, they cry a lot and quarrel with their girlfriends. Not really sure what they do, tell you the truth, Marmalade; I'm always too busy training.'

'Blimey!' said Marmalade. 'No wonder you don't get any goals.'

'That's another thing,' said Ron Drayne. 'People think football is all about goals. Football is *not* about goals! It's about commitment! It's about giving it hundred per cent! It's about . . .'

'Ron, cock,' said Marmalade.

'Yes?'

'Football *is* all about goals. And it's the *players* who have to be fit, not the manager.'

'Is it?' said Ron Drayne. 'And what makes you think that, little girl?'

'Look, if you kick the ball through their goal

and stop it going through your goal, you win every time. Don't you?'

Ron Drayne stared at Marmalade. The way she put it, it sounded very reasonable. He felt as if his whole world was turning upside down.

'No,' he said. 'It can't be that simple.'

'It *is* that simple, honest!'

'No, no, no, love. I've had a lifetime of experience of the game; I can't have little girls telling me how to do my job!'

'Suit yourself, cock,' said Marmalade. 'Only trying to help. Ask Rufus if you don't believe me. He's had more experience than anyone in the world, haven't you, Rufus?'

'I been around a bit,' said Rufus modestly.

During his short acquaintance with Rufus, Ron Drayne had formed a great affection and respect for him. With his wise old eyes peering from under his shaggy eyebrows, Rufus reminded Ron Drayne of his dear old manager from the days when he had started his playing career. Old Buzz Matby, the wisest, kindest man in the game. Tears sprang to Ron Drayne's eyes.

'Is she right, Mr Rufus?' he said.

'She is, Ron,' said Rufus. 'She's a daft young filly in some respects, but in this case she's right on the button. Tell you something else, Ron Drayne. You take life too serious. You want to have some fun and put yourself about a bit. You want to go clubbing yourself now and then.'

'Er, right, Mr Rufus,' said Ron Drayne respectfully. 'I'll bear it in mind.'

'Don't just bear it in mind, *do* it!' said Rufus firmly. 'We'll all go down the El Poko tonight. Strut our stuff, right? Right, that's enough talking. I got things to do.'

Ron Drayne stared in awe and respect as Rufus mooched off to patrol his territory.

'See you tonight, Ron,' said Marmalade Atkins.

At midnight, Marmalade woke and sat up in bed. She could hear shuffling and muttering and a few creaks and bumps, and for a moment she thought it was burglars, but then she heard Rufus's wheezy laugh and remembered. She tiptoed downstairs, and there in the lounge were Rufus and Ron Drayne. Ron Drayne looked very nervous, but Rufus was lolling about on the sofa, quite at his ease, watching the late-night movie.

'Thought you was never coming, young Marmalade. Nip upstairs and get three of your dad's ties; they got a dress code at El Poko, you know.'

Marmalade crept back up the stairs and into her parents' bedroom. The wardrobe door creaked as she opened it, and Mr Atkins turned over in his sleep and muttered: 'Honestly, Officer, I have a complete and innocent explanation,' then subsided into snoring again.

Marmalade selected an Old Etonian tie, an Old Harrovian tie, and a Garrick Club tie. (Mr Atkins had never been or belonged to any of these, but he felt that wearing the ties gave his customers a feeling of security.) She took them down to Ron Drayne and Rufus, and they all put them on.

'D'you think they'll let us in?' asked Marmalade doubtfully. They looked at themselves in the mirror: one girl in pyjamas and an Old Etonian tie; one worried-looking baldy with a false moustache and glasses, wearing a muddy tracksuit, trainers, and an Old Harrovian tie; and one dirty old ginger donkey wearing nothing at all except a Garrick Club tie.

'Course they will,' said Rufus. 'I'm well known at El Poko's.'

Marmalade had been to the El Poko once before, a long time ago ... or had she dreamed it? It certainly looked posh, with its glittering neon lights, its car park full of large, shiny cars, and its enormous bouncer in evening dress at the door, who was already glaring at them and spitting on his hands in anticipation of a nice bit of violence and intimidation.

'Leave this to me,' said Rufus, leading the way to the entrance.

'Evenin', son!' he said to the bouncer.

''Op it!' said the bouncer. 'No tracksuits, no pyjamas, no little girls and no donkeys. Smart dress only.'

'We're the cabaret, son,' said Rufus. 'I'm Good-Time Rufus, the Talking Donkey. I sings a bit as well.'

'A likely tale!' said the bouncer. 'Whoever heard of a talking donkey?'

'All right, we admit it. You're cleverer than you look, Sunny Jim. I'm not really a talking donkey – the little girl's a ventriloquist.'

The bouncer looked dubious. 'Who's your scruffy friend then?' he growled.

'He's our manager,' said Marmalade.

'No, that I cannot believe,' said the bouncer. 'Get out of here, the lot of you, before I throw you out!' And he gave Rufus a hard shove in the chest.

'You must be new to the bouncing game, Sunny Jim,' said Rufus, nudging the bouncer in the middle of his sparkling white evening shirt. The bouncer fell over backwards and Rufus stepped on to his chest and looked around in a puzzled way. 'Where did the geezer in the penguin suit go?' he said.

'He's on the floor,' said Marmalade.

'So he is,' said Rufus. 'Funny class of bouncer they're getting these days. Right, come on, lads. Let's put ourselves about and have a bit of fun.'

Rufus, Marmalade and Ron Drayne had a very good time at El Poko Nightclub and Restaurant. Rufus ate the flowers off all the tables, as well as some potted plants and decorative ferns, but the manager didn't seem to mind and the customers all thought he was extremely amusing. Marmalade and Ron Drayne both had treble sausage and chips ('On the house, naturally!' said the manager), and then all the other customers started cheering and shouting 'We want Good-Time Rufus!'

The manager came over and bowed respectfully. 'Would you mind, sir, as a very special favour?'

'Mind what?' said Ron Drayne in a panic.

'Don't worry, Ron,' said Rufus. 'It's me he wants.'

'There will of course be a large fee,' said the manager.

'Go on, Rufus,' said Marmalade. 'You know you like it.'

The manager handed Rufus a battered old straw hat, the orchestra struck up, and Rufus took the stage to roars of applause. He did all his old favourite numbers like 'I want to Eat Hay with You' and 'Don't let that Farmer Ride on Your Back!' This last one was a novelty number in which members of the audience were invited up on to the stage to see if they could mount and ride the Bucking Donkey – of course, none of them could. At one particular table a group of young men in smart Italian suits kept egging each other on to ride Rufus, but one by one they were tossed into a squirming heap at the back of the stage.

Finally Rufus beckoned to Ron Drayne, who came up very shyly, took the microphone, and sang 'My Way'. This went very well until the end, when he became so moved by his own singing that tears began to roll down his cheeks. As he raised his handkerchief to wipe them away, he wiped his false moustache and glasses off as well, and a great gasp echoed round the restaurant.

'That's Ron Drayne! Get him!'

The angry mob charged the stage to wreak vengeance on the disgraced England manager. Poor Ron Drayne couldn't move. He stood trembling, awaiting his fate, his eyes wide with terror.

Marmalade knew she had only a moment to do something.

'Get on his back and hold tight, Ron! Don't let go whatever happens! Rufus! Hee-haw Zig-zag!'

Ron Drayne clung tightly to Rufus's neck, and the scruffy old donkey reared up on his hind legs and let out a terrifyingly loud bray, a bit like the sound an elephant would make if it sat on a set of bagpipes. The clubbers scattered in all directions as Rufus zig-zagged round the tables, his eyes glaring and his huge yellow teeth bared. As he hurtled past Marmalade she managed to grab hold of the hood of Ron Drayne's tracksuit and hang on till they had gone through the main entrance and out into the cold night air of Warwickshire.

'Not a bad night, all things considered,' said Rufus. 'Enjoy that, did you, Ron?'

'Very much, till they recognised me,' said Ron Drayne rather mournfully. 'What am I going to do, Mr Rufus? How can I start a new life? All I know is football.'

'Don't worry,' said Marmalade. 'We're going to rebuild your career, starting tomorrow.'

'But how?'

'You're going to be the new Games Master at Hard Tack Hall,' said Marmalade.

Next day, Marmalade came down for breakfast and found her dad reading the paper. The main headline was RON'S GONE! over a report about the disappearance of the disgraced England manager. Down at the bottom of the page was a small item about another riot at the El Poko Nightclub and Restaurant.

'It says here, police are anxious to interview a ginger donkey in an Old Harrovian tie who was accompanied by a bald man in a tracksuit and a little girl in pyjamas!' said Mr Atkins. 'Well, well! The things folks get up to. Apparently some of the England team were in, and this donkey, or this bloke dressed in a donkey suit, threw them off the stage and gave them a bit of a kicking, then ran round shouting hee-haw, hee-haw!'

'Were those blokes in Italian suits from the *England team*?' said Marmalade.

'Doesn't say anything in here about Italian suits,' said Mr Atkins. He stared at his daughter suspiciously. 'What do you know about this, Marmalade?'

'Nothing, Daddy,' said Marmalade. 'I'm just an innocent little girl. Must dash now, or I'll be late for school! 'Bye, Daddy! 'Bye, Mumsy!' And off she skipped, swinging her satchel.

'I really think Hard Tack Hall has reformed our little girl, Muriel,' said Mr Atkins, as he selected his tie. Then he frowned. 'Funny!'

'What's funny, Atkins?'

'My Old Harrovian tie. It's all muddy and covered in ginger hairs!'

'Atkins! You haven't been sneaking off to see a *ginger girlfriend*, have you? Because if you have . . .'

'No! No! On my life, Muriel! I swear it!'

'Then I suspect *that girl* and her precious *donkey*!' said Mrs Atkins.

'Really?' said Mr Atkins. 'Surely not! What would a little girl and a donkey want with an Old Harrovian tie? No, Muriel, it will just have to remain one of life's unfathomable mysteries.'

'So you're applying for the job of Games Master, are you?' said Mr Suckling-Pygge.

'Yes, boss,' said Ron Drayne, trying to look keen.

'What's your name?'

'Er . . . Ron Brain, boss. Not to be confused with Ron Drayne, her-her-her!'

'No indeed!' said Mr Suckling-Pygge. 'Have you any testimonials?'

'Yes.'

'May I see them?'

'Um, um, um . . . unfortunately the dog chewed them up, boss.'

'This is not very satisfactory, Mr Brain. And, if I may say so, your appearance is distinctly on the scruffy side. You look as if you've been sleeping in straw!'

'He'll work without pay for the first week,' said Marmalade. 'Give him a trial, boss – I mean, cock – I mean, sir! You won't regret it.'

'Very well,' said Mr Suckling-Pygge, who liked something for nothing as much as the next man. 'We'll see how you shape up, Mr Brain. And as a special favour, you may borrow my shiny pink tracksuit.'

And that was how Ron Drayne got started on his great comeback as Ron Brain, the Back to Basics Football Wizard. His new philosophy was based on Mucking In and Getting the Ball in the Net, and his first step was Picking the Team.

'I want all the boys and girls out on the field please, Mr Suckling-Pygge,' he said.

'Girls do not play football, Mr Brain. Girls do embroidery.'

'Nothing in the rules about it,' said Ron

Drayne. 'Let's see how these girls shape up. I like the look of those four big ones.'

'You cannot turn my girl prefects into footballers!' shrieked Mr Suckling-Pygge, starting to jump up and down.

'We fancy football, don't we, girls?' said Monica.

'I absolutely forbid it!' squeaked Mr Suckling-Pygge.

Monica, Veronica, Japonica and Judy looked at each other. Then they picked up Mr Suckling-Pygge, carried him to his study, chained him to his chair, and locked him in. Having done that, they changed into football kit and went out on to the field. They were brilliant. All that practice in chasing Bad Girls and catching them and torturing them had made them very strong and fit. They struck terror into the hearts of most of the boys, and with Marmalade joining in with a few of her skinny-dodging runs and bendy-banana shots, they won the final of the five-a-side trial by twenty-three goals to nil.

'Ace footy, Watters!' said Norman Pratt. 'Me and Spratty are going to embroider a special School Banner to take to the Snobbe Towers match!'

Even Mr Suckling-Pygge was impressed when Marmalade unchained him and brought him out to see. 'The great secret of being a Back to Basics headmaster', he said, 'is knowing when to change your mind. I shall become famous as a pioneer of footy for girls! What a shame you're not a girl, Watkins! Ha, ha, ha!'

'As a matter of fact, cock, I *am* a girl,' said Marmalade.

'Now, now, Watkins, don't be silly,' said Mr Suckling-Pygge. 'So, Mr Brain, are we all ready for Snobbe Towers on Saturday?'

'Just about, boss,' said Ron Drayne. 'I've got the nucleus of a fine attacking side here. The only thing I haven't got is a goalie.'

'I'll get you a goalie,' said Marmalade.

The day of the great Schools' Cup Match was Saturday. Marmalade came down for breakfast and found her father reading the paper again.

'Strange, the twists of fate,' he said. 'Now he's gone they want him back again.'

Marmalade looked at the headline: COME BACK, RON – ALL IS FORGIVEN! The article underneath was all about how the England team was even worse without Ron Drayne than it had been with him. The lads had just gone down three-nil to Outer Mongolia in a friendly match, and next week was the final World Cup qualifier.

'Tragic, innit?' said Marmalade's dad. 'I almost feel like having a go at the job myself.'

'Don't be ridiculous, Atkins!' said his wife sternly. 'You've got quite enough to do without making a fool of yourself on a football pitch!

Aren't you supposed to be selling the Houses of Parliament this morning?'

'Quite right, Muriel; slipped me mind. No rest for the wicked, eh, Marmalade?'

The boys of Snobbe Towers arrived in a fleet of chauffeur-driven Rolls-Royces. Most of them were the sons of dukes and earls and million-aires, and thought themselves far too grand to be playing football with oiks from Hard Tack Hall, especially when they got out on the foot-ball pitch and found that half the team were girls.

'*Girls*? We can't play football with *girls*!' fluted the Honourable Lord Archibald Arbuthnot, cap-tain of the Snobbe Towers team.

'Nothing about girls in the rule book, cock,' said Marmalade.

'So yah boo sucks to you!' said Norman Pratt bravely.

Just then there was a ripple of amazement and laughter from the crowd as a shaggy ginger figure trotted out on to the pitch and stood between the goalposts. Marmalade had been unable to find a pair of shorts big enough to fit over Rufus's large rump, but she had managed to get Porpoise Perkins's black and white football shirt over his head. He was a pretty fearsome sight as he bared his yellow teeth and reared up on his hind legs, displaying his hairy, mud-encrusted belly.

'*Donkeys*? We can't play football with *donkeys*!' said Lord Archibald.

'Nothing about donkeys in the rule book, cock,' said Marmalade.

'So yah boo sucks to you!' said Norman Spratt.

Ron Drayne gave the team a short tactical talk embodying his new Back to Basics football philosophy: kick the ball in their goal a lot and don't let them kick it in your goal at all. Then Mr Suckling-Pygge blew the whistle and the game was on.

An hour and a half later, the snobs of Snobbe Towers dove off in their Rolls-Royces in tears and in disgrace. Hard Tack Hall had won by twenty-two goals to nil. Monica had scored two goals, Veronica three, Japonica four, and Judy had gone berserk and scored six before being sent off for tying Lord Archibald to the goalposts with his own bootlaces. Marmalade scored five, and even Pratty and Spratty got one each. And just before the final whistle, Rufus, who had been feeling left out, did a hee-haw zig-zag all the way down the pitch, finishing up with the ball and half the Snobbe Towers team entangled in the netting.

Mr Suckling-Pygge was terribly excited. His new Games Master had really put Hard Tack Hall on the map – and in the headlines. The headmaster gave interviews all over the place, to newspapers and on radio and even on television, smirking and preening into the camera and telling everyone how Back to Basics Football was the key to Making Britain Great again.

And Back to Basics Football really did seem to be working. All the best football teams rolled up in their coaches, determined to teach Hard Tack Hall a lesson and making sarcastic remarks about girls and donkeys, but they all went away with their tails between their legs. Soon all the football writers were coming to watch Hard Tack Hall matches and sing the praises of the brilliant Ron Brain and his wonderful team of world-beaters. After that the headlines started to appear:

NEW WONDER RON
BRAIN OF BRITAIN!
GIVE RON THE JOB!

One day, a telegram arrived at Hard Tack Hall, inviting Ron Brain to take over as England manager.

'This is the proudest day in my life,' he said to Marmalade and Rufus. 'And I owe it all to you.'

'Think nothing of it, cock,' said Marmalade.

'I don't know how I'll get along without you,' said Ron Drayne, tears rolling down his cheeks and wetting his false moustache.

'You won't have to,' said Marmalade. 'We're coming too.'

*

The England squad did their training at a very posh hotel called the Hightowers Health Hydro. The Hightowers Health Hydro had a gym and a swimming pool and a cross-country course, but it also had a nightclub and a bar and a slap-up restaurant, and that was where the England squad did most of their training. They trained so hard that they could stay up all night for weeks on end, drink like fish, and eat like hippopotamuses. They had already been there for a week when Ron Brain and his assistants arrived, and by then most of them were bursting the buttons on their smart Italian suits. Ron and Marmalade and Rufus stared at them in dismay as they lolled by the swimming pool like a colony of elephant seals, groaning and burping and occasionally flopping into the water. And the England squad stared at Ron and Marmalade and Rufus.

'Here, lads,' said Bozza Brown, once famous for his twinkle-toed agility, now famous only for the size of his belly. 'This isn't a new Ron, that's a what-you-call – a continuation of the old Ron by other means. And there's that ginger tosser had a go at us down the Poko that night.'

'Oh, yeah,' said Vinny Nutbutter, blinking. 'He's a right tosser, him; tossed you off the stage for a start, her-her-her!'

'And there's that nasty little shrimp; she was there in her pyjamas and her dad's tie. Let's get 'em, lads!'

But Bozza and Vinny were so gross and bloated that they could barely get up, and when they did manage to stand upright and lurch menacingly towards Marmalade and Rufus, they were quite out of breath by the time they reached them. Rufus gave them each a gentle nudge, and they plopped into the pool like a couple of giant goldfish.

'How can I build a winning team out of this lot?' said Ron in despair.

'I think we'd better send for the prefects,' said Marmalade.

Bozza Brown, Vinny Nutbutter and the rest of the England layabouts had never had to deal with anything like the Hard Tack Hall prefects. Monica, Veronica, Japonica and Judy chased them mercilessly round and round the hotel grounds all day and chained them to the machines in the gym at night; and by the end of the week they were lean and fit enough to button up all the buttons on their flash Italian suits, and even – which was more to the point – get into their football shorts.

'Right, lads,' said Ron Drayne. 'Tactics.'

'We know the tactics,' said Bozza Brown. 'Pose about looking dead moody and dangerous. Football is not about goals.'

'No, lads, we've got new Back to Basics tactics: kick the ball in their goal a lot, and don't let them kick it in your goal at all.'

Bozza and Vinny looked totally dumb-founded. 'What about kicking the other team like, boss, and nutting them and that?'

'No, Vinny,' said Ron proudly. 'We're trying this new thing now: we don't kick *them*, we kick the ball!'

Vinny and Bozza scratched their heads. 'It'll never catch on, boss,' said Bozza.

But it did catch on. Thanks to the strict discipline provided by Monica, Veronica, Japonica and Judy, and Ron Drayne's revolutionary new Back to Basics Football philosophy, the fortunes of the England team revived. They even started to win matches. In the return game with Outer Mongolia, they won by six goals to one. They then drew with Holland, beat China and just scraped home in extra time against Germany (Rufus did a hee-haw zig-zag down the touchline and the German centre-forward missed a penalty kick), and that put them in the Final of the World Cup against Italy.

Ron Drayne gave a press conference in which he revealed the truth: that the old Ron Drayne and the new Ron Brain were one and the same person, and that he owed his comeback to the brilliant brains of Marmalade and Rufus Atkins.

'Makes you proud, don't it, Muriel?' said Mr Atkins to his wife, as they sat watching their huge gold-plated television set. 'Our little girl, that is. We must have done something right, eh?'

'Atkins,' said his wife, whacking him absent-mindedly but firmly on the head with a champagne bottle, 'you are a self-deluding idiot (*whack!*). This sordid episode will end in grief, mark my words (*whack!*), like all the others (*whack!*). That girl was sent to torment us and make our lives a mockery (*whack!*). So pass the chocolates, Atkins, and shut up (*whack!*)!'

'You know what, Muriel?' said Mr Atkins, wishing he had a motorcycle helmet for indoor wear. 'I think I might nip along to Wembley and take a gander at the Final. Lot of foreign visitors – I might even be able to do a bit of business.'

The day of the World Cup Final dawned. Every ticket had been sold, as well as several hundred forged ones that Mr Atkins had run up on Marmalade's Bad Girl's Printing Set. Everybody wanted to see whether Ron Drayne's revitalised team could penetrate the celebrated Italian defence. The Italian manager, Signor Michelangelo Machiavelli, had invented a superbly cunning system called the Muro Defensivo – the Defensive Wall. Every time the other side got the ball, the Italian team would all crowd together in front of goal in a human wall. No one could get the ball past them. They had not conceded a single goal in the whole competition.

And so it proved in the Final. Marmalade and Rufus were sitting in their specially reserved seats on the manager's bench. Marmalade was wearing a pair of knitted ear-muffs, because football managers get very excited at important matches and use words that are not fit for the ears of little girls.

Rufus didn't bother with any ear-muffs. It takes a lot to shock a donkey. He was muttering a few bad words himself, as a matter of fact. He didn't like Wembley Stadium much. 'Call this a field?' he grumbled. 'They mown it too short. Donkey can't get a proper chew at it. They wants to stop all this footballing and let the grass grow, that's what I says.'

A great roar went up, followed by a groan as yet another shot crashed into the Italian Muro Defensivo and rebounded harmlessly. It was five minutes from time and the score was still nil-nil, when suddenly Vinny Nutbutter cracked up with the frustration of it all, head-butted the goal-post, and knocked himself out cold. Bozza Brown burst into inconsolable tears as he saw his best friend being stretchered off, and had to leave the field too.

'Marmalade! Rufus!' said Ron Drayne. 'You're on.'

The Italian fans roared with laughter when Rufus and Marmalade took the pitch. '*E arrivata la piccola ragazza! E arrivato il ano inglese! Quello stupido spectaculo!*'

61

'I never liked walls much,' said Rufus to Marmalade. 'Or fences. Shall I kick 'em in the back of the net?'

'Think that's against the rules,' said Marmalade. 'I've got another idea.'

The ball went over the touchline, and Marmalade ran to take the throw-in. All the Italian team rushed back to goal and got into their wall formation. You couldn't see any of the goal at all – just a solid mass of Italian muscle. Marmalade threw the ball to Rufus on the halfway line.

'Hold it there till I shout,' she yelled. 'Come on, boys – new tactics!'

She trotted up to the Italian Defensive Wall and grinned at them. There was one minute to go. She chose the biggest and broadest Italian defender, Gluteo Maximo.

'Are you ticklish, cock?' she said.

'What you mean, little girl?' said Gluteo Maximo. 'What is this "ticklish"?'

'Well,' said Marmalade, going up close, 'some people are ticklish if you go eedly-weedly under their arms like that . . .'

'Stop, stop, little girl! *Basta, ragazza!*' squealed Gluteo, who was very ticklish indeed.

'And some people are ticklish if you go wagga-wagga-wagga round their ribs like that,' said Marmalade.

'*Aiuto me! Aiuto me!* Help!' squealed Gluteo. It was all too much for him and he collapsed on the ground in a paroxysm of giggles, bringing

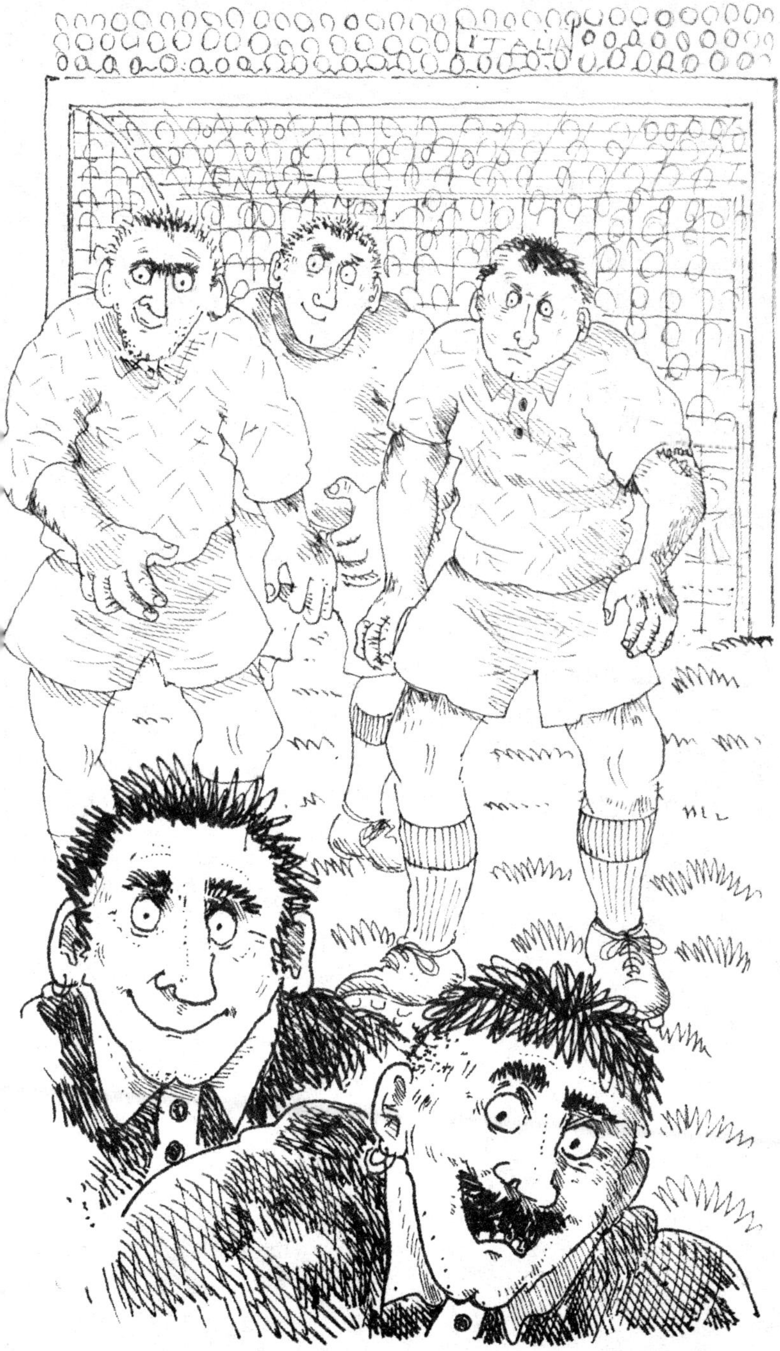

down the rest of the Defensive Wall with him. Ten seconds to go.

'Back heel, Rufus!' yelled Marmalade. Rufus turned his back on the ball and lashed out with his back leg. He had practised this kick on countless post office vans and millionaires' Mercedes. The ball flew like a rocket into the back of the Italian net, and the final whistle blew. England had won the World Cup!

Except that when it was time to present it, the World Cup was nowhere to be seen. Apparently a man in a pork-pie hat and a camel-hair overcoat, calling himself the Duke of Warwickshire, had said he was just borrowing it for five minutes to show his friend Lord Watkins, and had then driven off with it.

Ron Drayne was desolated. 'All my life', he said, 'I've been waiting for this moment. The World Cup. And now someone's nicked it.'

'Never mind, cock,' said Marmalade. 'It's only a game.'

Marmalade at Oxford

'Whatever has happened to the art of letter-writing? That's what I ask myself,' said Mr Atkins, crumpling up another envelope and tossing it into the World Cup trophy, which sat proudly in the centre of the Atkinses' mantelpiece. 'I must have opened ten letters this morning, and none of them have been any good. Dissatisfied customers asking for their money back, threatening letters from solicitors, bills, begging letters . . . hello! This one looks a bit different. It's about our Marmalade.'

'Oh, Atkins!' shrieked Marmalade's mother. 'Has someone made us an offer for her at last? I *knew* reducing her to fifty pence would do the trick. People will buy any old rubbish if the price is right!'

'No, no,' said Mr Atkins. 'It's better than that. It's from Oxford University.' He picked up the letter and read it out loud: ' "From the Principal, Goodness Gracious College, Oxford. Dear Mr Atkins, we are pleased to be able to offer your daughter Marmalade one of our special Scholarships for Bad but Interesting girls." '

'Is there any *cash* involved, Atkins?' asked his wife.

'Three thousand nicker, non-returnable!'

'Then write without delay and tell them we accept! You can buy a lot of chocs for three thousand nicker. The World Cup is all very well, but cash is cash and not to be sneezed at!'

'Look, hang on, Mother,' said Marmalade, coming downstairs. 'If you carry on like this I'll get the feeling you're trying to get rid of me.'

'We *are* trying to get rid of you!' shrieked Mrs Atkins. 'We've been trying for years!'

'Well, I don't want to go to Oxford. It's full of swots and snobs and upper-class twits. Why can't I stay at Hard Tack Hall? I was just settling down there.'

'Afraid they don't agree, Marmalade. I've got a letter here from that Mr Pigsucker or whatever he calls himself – Suckling-Pygge, that's right. Says he's afraid you're the unacceptable face of Back to Basics. Says you've given him two identity crises and a nervous breakdown. Says his shiny pink tracksuit will never be the same again. I'm afraid it's Oxford or nothing, Marmalade,' said Mr Atkins.

'Oh, all right then. I'll give it a whirl,' said Marmalade. 'Can I take Rufus?'

'Don't be ridiculous, darling,' said Mrs Atkins. 'Whoever heard of a *donkey* going to *university*?'

A week later, one small girl and one ginger donkey arrived at Oxford University. The streets were thronged with weedy youths clutching their teddy bears and tossing their golden locks about.

'Oh, look!' cried the weediest-looking one of the lot. 'What a perfectly sweet little donkey! May I give him a stroke?'

'Please do!' said Marmalade. 'If you don't mind him giving you a kick.'

The weedy youth advanced on Rufus, who looked rather alarmed, and sneezed violently.

'Oh, the poor sweetie! Has it got a cold?'

'No,' said Marmalade. 'It's the pong of your blinking aftershave probably.'

'Well, I do like to be fragrant. Lord Sebastian's the name, by the way,' said the slender youth, reaching out timidly to touch Rufus's tatty old mane. 'My! How deliciously rough and shaggy!'

Rather to Marmalade's surprise, Rufus didn't give Lord Sebastian a kick, or even a hard nudge. He just blinked once or twice and looked rather pleased and bashful.

'I think he likes you, cock,' said Marmalade.

'Oh, goody! Are we to be bosom pals, then?'

'Looks like it,' said Marmalade. 'Oh, I'm Lord Marmalade and he's Lord Rufus, by the way. We're looking for Goodness Gracious College.'

'Really! How absolutely topping! That's my college too! It's just down here,' said Lord Sebastian.

As they picked their way through the

quaint old streets, Lord Sebastian pointed out the sights: the dreaming spires, the grumpy policemen listening to opera on their personal radios, and students, students everywhere. Some of the students were like Lord Sebastian – weedy youths with teddies and golden curls; and some of them were quite different – great roaring brutes with red faces and cans of lager. Lord Sebastian explained that they were called the Hearties and that his lot were called the Softies.

'They hate us, Marmalade. I don't know why. We get right up their noses. I think it's because we don't like sports and they're sporty types. They wreck our rooms and sometimes they debag us, you know.'

'What's that then, cock?' said Marmalade.

"Well," said Lord Sebastian, going rather pink, "it means they chase us and pull our trousers off."

'What do they do that for?' said Marmalade.

'Nobody knows. It's just one of those traditional Oxford customs.'

'Well, they won't debag Lord Marmalade and Lord Rufus, cock!' said Marmalade.

'Lord Rufus hasn't *got* any bags, have you, pet?' said Lord Sebastian. 'He's naked as nature intended!'

Rufus looked embarrassed and gave Lord Sebastian a quick kick up the backside that sent him sprawling in the gutter.

'I say, what was that for?' said Lord Sebastian, as Marmalade helped him up.

'He doesn't like folk taking liberties,' said Marmalade. 'Anyway, he's not naked as nature intended; he's got his own coat.'

'Sorry,' said Lord Sebastian. 'I didn't mean to be rude; I'm just a bit of a twit, I'm afraid. No offence meant, Lord Rufus.'

'None taken,' said Rufus in his hoarse, gruff tones.

'Oh, I'm so relieved. Well, here we are – Goodness Gracious College!'

Goodness Gracious College was a beautiful old building with an arched gateway that opened out into a lovely courtyard with a square of succulent green grass in the middle. Rufus was a bit hot and tired after his journey. When horses and donkeys are hot and sweaty, there's nothing they like better than a good roll on the grass, and when Rufus saw the beautiful quadrangle of Goodness Gracious College, he galumphed through the arch past the astonished porter, ran right into the middle of the quad, and rolled about on his back, kicking his legs in the air.

'Ho!' said the porter. 'We can't have that! Get that animal out of here! Only the dons are allowed on that grass!'

'What's a don?' Marmalade asked Lord Sebastian.

'Oh, it's just what they call the teachers here.'

'Do they roll on the grass then?'

'Er . . . not usually.'

'Look here, shorty!' roared the porter. 'Are you going to get that animal off the sacred turf or not?'

'Certainly not,' said Marmalade. 'And less of the shorty, if you don't mind. I don't call you fatty, do I, fatty? Ooh, I just did! Never mind, eh, cock? Now listen to me. That animal, as you call him, is Lord Rufus Atkins, and he *does* happen to be a don. Well, he's a don*key*, anyway, and that's even better. Stands to reason. By the way, did anyone ever tell you you've got a face like a hippopotamus?'

'I *beg* your pardon?' said the porter, quivering all over with rage.

'*Deaf hippopotamus*,' said Marmalade. 'I always think the old jokes are best, don't you, cock? Now pick up my bags and take me to your leader!'

'And who might you be, small and vociferous young person?' The voice was deep and thundery. Marmalade looked up to see a huge old man with a long grey beard, wearing a mortarboard and with a great black gown flapping round his ankles.

'Marmalade Atkins, cock. Who are you?'

The huge old man stuck his thumbs in his gown, waggled his hairy eyebrows, and roared in fearsome tones.

'I am the great Professor Blowitt,
What there is to know, I know it,
What I don't know, isn't knowledge;
And I am Master of this College!'

'Please to meet you, cock,' said Marmalade. 'I am just a little oik, and mucking about is what I loike!'

'Excellent! Excellent! I surmise you must be our new scholar, the Bad but Interesting Girl!'

'Correct, cock,' said Marmalade.

'And, er, that . . .?' Professor Blowitt inclined his head towards Rufus, who was still lying on his back with his legs in the air, but had stopped rolling and indeed appeared to be asleep.

'My colleague,' said Marmalade. 'Professor Rufus. He a donkey expert. Been studying them so long he's even got to look like one!'

'Fascinating, fascinating! Well, make yourselves at home; we're all a bit eccentric here. Lord Sebastian will take you to your rooms, and then you must both be my guests at High Table for dinner!'

'Hope it's not *too* high,' said Marmalade. 'I'm only four foot eight.'

Lord Sebastian led Marmalade and Rufus up the narrow winding staircase to their rooms, where they unpacked their bags. Rufus didn't have much in his bag – just some oats, and he'd eaten most of those on the way. Then they changed into their evening dress (bow tie for Rufus) and went down to dinner in the Great Hall of Goodness Gracious College.

It all looked very grand. There was one High Table on a sort of stage, where all the professors and other big nobs sat, and down below in the Main Hall there were ten Low Tables full of students – four tables of Softies with their teddies (some of the teddies were even wearing bow ties and bibs) and five tables of horrible great big red-faced Hearties, all roaring like bulls and throwing bread at the Softies and the teddies.

High Table *was* very high, so high that Marmalade could hardly get her chin over it. Rufus was all right because he always ate his dinner standing up. After a bit Marmalade got fed up with asking the professors to pass her things because none of them took any notice; they were all far too busy feeding their own faces and boasting about all the great books they had written. So she climbed on the table and helped herself to fish and chips. None of the professors took any notice, but a great shout went up from all the red-faced Hearties.

'I say, chaps! There's a frightful little oik crawling about on High Table! Let's throw bread at it!'

A great shower of bread cascaded on to High Table, and all the professors got very excited and started to throw it back, together with walnuts, sardines, cod, chips and anything they could lay their hands on.

Marmalade and Rufus got under the table and ate their dinner there in peace, while the battle raged over their heads.

'These students and professors are all barmy,' said Marmalade.

'Too much studying and book reading,' said Rufus. 'Turns folks' heads into mush. They looks all right on the outside, but inside – all full of mush. No use to man or beast.'

'And that's with studying and book reading, is it?'

'That's it, young Marmalade. So mind you don't do none of it while you're here.'

'I'd better just Muck About, hadn't I?' said Marmalade.

'That's it. Stick to what you know, and you won't go wrong.'

So when Marmalade had finished her fish and chips, she tied all the professors' shoelaces together under the table, and then she and Rufus sneaked off to bed.

Some time later, when the Great Bread Fight was over, the professors rose from the table to make their way to the Senior Common Room for more port and nuts, but as their shoelaces were tied together, they all fell over in a great heap.

'How very strange!' said Professor Blowitt. 'What are we all doing down here?'

'I thought you were supposed to know everything, Blowitt,' said Professor Carp rather cunningly.

'Ho, well, I do really; I was just testing you,' said Professor Blowitt.

'I think it must have something to do with the Bad but Interesting Girl,' said Professor Carp.

'Yes, I believe you may be right. Hard to be sure, of course, when you've got a head full of mush, but I shall speak to the Bad but Interesting Girl tomorrow.'

'Jolly good bread fight, though.'

'Oh, absolutely. Best for weeks.'

Next morning, Lord Sebastian called bright and early to take Marmalade and Rufus punting on the river. If you haven't been to Oxford, you may not know what punting is. It's a very nice way of wasting a hot summer's day, and it gives you a very good chance of falling in the river and getting wet all over. A punt is a flat-bottomed boat, and you move it along by pushing a long pole against the river bottom. It's a lot harder than it looks. Fortunately Lord Sebastian was very good at it, despite being a Softie. He got Rufus to sit in the middle of the punt and gave him his teddy to look after. Marmalade sat right at the front to keep a look-out, and Sebastian himself stood up at the back and pushed off.

'This be the loife, Marmalade!' said Rufus, as the punt glided along the smooth silvery water and under the shady overhanging trees.

'Can I have a go with the pole thing?' said Marmalade.

'Er . . . well, OK, if you're sure you can manage it,' said Lord Sebastian a little doubtfully. 'But what am I saying? Life should be one big adventure, shouldn't it?'

'It usually is with her,' said Rufus.

Marmalade and Lord Sebastian changed places, crawling very carefully past Rufus. The punt wobbled ominously, but Marmalade scrambled to the stern, picked up the pole, and stood up shakily.

'Here we go!' she yelled, driving the pole in hard. The punt shot forward, the pole stuck in the mud at the bottom of the river, and Marmalade was left stranded, hanging on top of the pole, while Rufus and Lord Sebastian floated briskly away from her down river.

'Oi! Come back!' yelled Marmalade, but they didn't have any way of getting back, or steering themselves because she had the pole. Swaying about on top of it, she watched them vanishing under Magdalen Bridge.

Suddenly, behind her, Marmalade heard a

series of little splashes and hoarse, rhythmic grunts. Someone was yelling 'In! Out! In! Out! One . . . Two . . . Three . . .' and on 'Three' she was catapulted off the end of the pole, and did a triple somersault in the air. She held her nose and got ready for the big splash, but to her amazement she crashed down on a little fat man in a dark blue blazer, who went: 'In! Out! In! Out! Aaaaargh!'

Marmalade had bombed on the Oxford Boat Race crew!

The little fat man she had landed on was called Pogo Smith-Parsons, and he was the cox of the crew. In a boat race, the cox is the little man (or woman) who sits at the back of the boat doing the steering and yelling at the big guys who do the real work. Not a bad job, all things considered. Pogo Smith-Parsons wasn't enjoying it too much at the moment. He had a sore neck because Marmalade was sitting astride his shoulders and he couldn't see anything because she had her hands over his eyes.

'Wow!' said Marmalade. 'This is brilliant!'

They flashed past the drifting punt with Lord Sebastian and Lord Rufus on it. Rufus let out a loud 'Hee-haw!' and then they were gone, dots into the distance.

'We're going into the bank!' yelled Marmalade.

'Pull on the rope!' screeched Pogo Smith-Parsons.

'Which one?' yelled Marmalade.

Pogo Smith-Parsons made no reply, possibly because he had Marmalade's foot in his mouth, and the Oxford boat turned a sharp left and slithered up the bank, finishing up in the middle of a rather quaint open-air café.

'Just the job,' said Marmalade. 'Anybody fancy an ice cream?'

That night, while Marmalade and Rufus were lolling about in their rooms eating a plateful of jam rolls and a nosebag full of carrots, they heard the trampling of heavy feet on the staircase, and a thunderous knocking on the door. Marmalade went to open it, and there stood the Oxford boat crew: eight enormous Hearties, all about two metres tall and one metre wide.

'Atkins,' said the Captain of boats, who was called Trevor Thicke, 'you are a jumped-up little oik, but we like your style. More to the point, you are practically a midget. How would you like to cox the Oxford crew in the Boat Race?'

'What about your pal Pogo Smith-Parsons?' asked Marmalade.

'We're fed up with Pogo,' said the crew. 'Always yelling at us. *And* he's got all fat and heavy. Too many cream buns and too many lagers. We want a nice skinny little girlie who'll do what she's told.'

'Gosh, boys, that's a terrific honour!' said Marmalade shyly.

'Yah, well, we think you're brill really,' said Trevor Thicke, shifting from foot to foot in an embarrassed way. As he weighed about 150 kilos, the floorboards began to creak ominously and all the pictures fell off the walls.

'You see, the thing is, Atkins, we all went to Eton and places like that, and we don't know much about girls, yah?' said Trevor Thicke. 'But we think you're brill and excellent, yah, and we'd – you know – we'd love to have you in the boat.'

'Gosh, boys,' said Marmalade. 'I think you're all really sweet.' *All* the Oxford boat crew went pink in the face and started to shift about from foot to foot.

'No, no, boys, one at a time, please!' screeched Marmalade. Too late. The venerable floorboards gave way with a squeak and a creak and a crumble and a great crash, and Trevor Thicke, the Oxford boat crew, Marmalade and Rufus, all fell through into the floor below.

Rufus was most annoyed, and had to gallop three times round the Sacred Turf before he could calm down, but the Oxford crew were so tough and so thick they hardly noticed anything unusual. They were always falling through things and off things and out of things. Trevor Thicke clambered to his feet and started to brush himself down.

'Well, um, Marmalade,' he said. 'That was

really – you know – really great. See you in the boat tomorrow, yah?'

'Oh, yah, Trevor!' said Marmalade.

The days went by. Every morning, Marmalade jumped out of bed at the crack of dawn, tied on her Dark Blue Oxford headband, and went down to the river to train with Trevor Thicke and his Hearties. She went 'Yah!' and she went 'Rah, rah, rah!' and she stayed up late and threw bread with the chaps. It seemed that the impossible had happened: Marmalade Atkins had become a horrid posh girlie.

Rufus and Lord Sebastian became depressed, and Lord Sebastian's teddy started to lose his fur. 'He's all stressed out,' said Lord Sebastian. 'You'll be losing your mane next, Rufus.'

They watched gloomily as the boat flashed past, going faster than it had ever gone before, with the brilliant new super-lightweight girlie cox. 'In! Out! In! Out! Rah! Rah! Rah! That's it chaps! Super! Ten more big ones for your favour-ite girlie!' went Marmalade, and Rufus turned away disgusted.

'I can't stick no more of this,' he said. 'I'm going home.'

Marmalade was dismayed that night when she found the muddy note on her pillow. It said: 'Now you are a good gurl and no muckin about you wont want me no more so cheerio from R Atkins.'

'Oh, *Rufus*!' she wailed, although he wasn't there to hear her. 'I'm not really a Horrid Posh Girlie, I was just waiting for my big chance!'

The next day was the day of the Oxford and Cambridge Boat Race, which is not held at Oxford or Cambridge but along the Thames in London. All the posh snobs in England go along in their stripy blazers and straw hats with ribbons and cheer and shout and squirt champagne at each other and fall out of their motor boats.

Marmalade found herself the Star Girlie Cox of the fastest Oxford crew ever. The Cambridge crew looked just as big and stupid, but their cox wasn't so skinny, which gave Oxford an advantage.

Some way down the river, a tall and willowy figure was leaning droopily over the balustrade of Hammersmith Bridge, tears rolling down his aristocratic cheeks and soaking his teddy. Lord Sebastian was waiting for a last glimpse of his ex-friend Marmalade. Suddenly he heard a loud snort, and felt something rough and hairy pushing against the back of his neck. He turned round, and there was Rufus.

'Rufus, my dear chap!' said Lord Sebastian, wiping his eyes with a silk handkerchief. 'I thought you'd gone for ever! What are you doing here?'

Rufus made no reply, but stuck his head on

one side and closed one eye. He had thought of a plan.

Meanwhile, back at the starting line, the two boats lined up next to each other. Both the crews were very tense. Trevor Thicke leaned forward and whispered to Marmalade, 'I just want to say, whatever happens, I think you are a super girlie and I wish you were my girlfriend.'

YUCK!

Marmalade just stopped herself from being sick over the side of the boat, then the starter's pistol went, and they were off. 'In! Out! In! Out! Rah! Rah! Rah!' went Marmalade, and as the two crews approached Hammersmith Bridge, Oxford were starting to edge ahead.

Then a familiar scruffy ginger silhouette reared up over the balustrade and let out a magnificent 'Hee-haw!' It was Rufus. The Cambridge cox let go of the tiller and his boat veered dangerously towards Marmalade's.

'Rufus!' yelled Marmalade. 'I thought you'd broken friends with me! Come and join us! Come on! There's plenty of room!'

With another great 'Hee-haw!' Rufus leapt over the balustrade scattering the posh snobs. He seemed to hover in the air for several seconds before landing with his front legs in the Oxford boat, and his back legs in the Cambridge boat.

You might have seen the famous Boat Race in which one of the boats sank. Well, this was the year when *both* boats sank. Both crews floundered around in the water, gasping and spluttering, while all the motor boats crashed into each other, most of them capsizing as well.

Marmalade and Rufus paddled companiably to the shore.

'Jolly brill boat race, yah?' said Marmalade.

'I likes messing about on the river,' said Rufus.

Down Under

'Marmalade Atkins,' boomed Professor Blowitt, 'you and your . . . *ginger colleague* have brought Oxford University into disrepute! You are a disgrace to Goodness Gracious College!'

It has to be said that Marmalade and Rufus didn't look much of a credit to Goodness Gracious College. They were both soaking wet, for a start, standing in two muddy puddles (one large, one small) on Professor Blowitt's precious antique carpet.

Rufus's new sport of jumping off bridges on to boats had caught on in a big way, and Marmalade and Rufus had been demonstrating it to lots of people who wanted to take it up, not to mention newspaper reporters and television crews. All over the country, quite respectable ladies and gentlemen were going completely barmy, roaring 'Hee-haw!' at the tops of their voices and throwing themselves off all sorts of bridges on to all sorts of boats and ships. The hospitals were full of squashed sailors and the whole thing had got completely out of hand.

'It's not our fault, cock,' said Marmalade. 'It was just, you know, one thing led to another. We didn't *mean* to sink the boats, did we, Rufus?'

Rufus stared out of the window and sighed a long wheezy sigh. There was a very succulent-looking fern in a pot in the corner of Professor Blowitt's study, just the sort of thing a donkey likes for a snack around eleven o'clock in the morning. A nice potted fern makes a very tasty second breakfast. It would only be polite if Professor Blowitt asked if there were any donkeys who fancied a nice snack of potted fern, thought Rufus. It didn't look as if anyone else was going to eat it, and it was a shame to see it going to waste. What Rufus didn't know was that this fern was a particularly rare and valuable specimen, brought by Professor Blowitt from the rain forests of the Andes for scientific study and analysis. Actually, it wouldn't have made a lot of difference to Rufus if he *had* known it. He didn't hold with studying plants, he held with eating them. He couldn't understand why folks would want to stand about talking when there were nice juicy ferns just sitting there waiting to be chomped up.

'I thought you *liked* Bad but Interesting Girls,' Marmalade was saying.

'Well, yes, yes, you have a point – but we didn't realise just how Bad and Interesting little girls could be,' said the Master of Goodness Gracious. 'Or . . . ah . . . donkeys.'

Rufus couldn't stand it any longer. A donkey could starve to death while folk were talking. Talking was almost as bad as studying and book reading, in his opinion. He had heard of donkeys whose hind legs had fallen off listening to folks talking. He hadn't actually seen it happen, but he wasn't about to take the risk. He walked over to the fern in the corner of the room and nibbled a bit. It tasted just as good as it looked.

'Professor Rufus! Please!' gasped Professor Blowitt. 'That is a unique and priceless specimen of *Phyllidilicus Marcuspensicus*!'

Rufus nibbled another bit. 'That so?' he said. 'Very tasty and all.'

All at once Professor Blowitt began to realise what a terrible mistake he had made allowing Marmalade and Rufus into the hallowed precincts of Goodness Gracious College. He could feel one of his rages coming on. He started to get very hot and agitated.

'Just leave that fern alone, you – you – horrible disgusting hairy ginger monstrosity!' he spluttered.

'Don't you talk to Rufus like that, cock!' said Marmalade. 'He's got feelings, same as you.'

'Just – just – just – get out of here!' spluttered the Professor.

Rufus grinned, showing his large yellow teeth. Then he opened his mouth wide and chomped up the rest of Professor Blowitt's unique and valuable fern. 'Just the job,' he said. 'Saved me life. Come on, young Marmalade; all these books and stuff give me the creeps. Afternoon, Professor. Very good of you to have us, but we likes the simple life.'

Lord Sebastian saw them off at the college gates with a big bunch of roses and a big box of chocolates. (Marmalade ate the chocolates and Rufus ate the roses.)

It felt very good to be going back home to Warwickshire. Mucking about with the posh snobs and professors had been all right for a bit, but Marmalade was worried that her parents might be missing her. Without her to keep them on the alert, they might sink into a decline. And Rufus had been missing the farm. The quad at Goodness Gracious College had been fine for rolling about on, but not like a proper field, with rough, tufty, long grass and tasty thistles and clover and proper big dandelions and nettles and all the kinds of things a donkey likes to get his teeth into. He'd been missing his girlfriend Jenny, too, even though he hadn't bothered to send so much as a postcard home. (All donkeys can read, and write too, if they want, as well as talk, but most of them strongly disapprove of all of these things. Jenny set no store at all by postcards. Gordon the billy goat was the only animal on the farm who liked postcards, and he only liked them to eat.)

Marmalade and Rufus were both looking forward to a nice quiet time at home, but as they approached the farm they saw Harry Hawk's small black van parked outside, and Harry Hawk himself standing beside it, with his beaky nose gleaming in the evening light and a little dewdrop glittering on the end of it. He grinned at Marmalade.

'Shouldn't you be at school, little girl?' he said.

'Do me a favour, cock,' said Marmalade. 'It's gone home time. And anyway, I'm a student now – just home for the weekend from Goodness Gracious College, Oxford. I'm a child prodigy, cock. And he's a donkey prodigy. So yah boo sucks!'

'Little girl,' said Harry Hawk, smiling his horrible smile, 'I happen to know you're *not* just home for the weekend. I happen to know they've chucked you out of Goodness Gracious. So let me ask you one simple question.'

'Let me ask *you* one simple question,' said Marmalade. 'Is that your nose, or are you trying to grow icicles on your bonce?'

Harry Hawk grinned. 'Oh, dear, the jokes *are* flying about this evening! I like to have a little joke now and then meself. Here, have you heard the latest? There's a new policy starting on Bad Little Girls. The idea is, *condemn 'em more and understand 'em less.*'

'What's that supposed to mean then?' said Marmalade.

'Ooh, I wouldn't know. Too deep for Harry Hawk, that one is. But I *have* heard of little girls condemned to twenty years' hard labour in Dartmoor Prison!'

'Wouldn't worry me, cock,' said Marmalade. 'Dartmoor's a doddle. I've *been* in Dartmoor.' She had, too. But that's another story . . .

'Well,' said Harry Hawk, grinning, 'no doubt we'll be able to think of something less to your taste. I was reading in the paper they've discovered this new scientific technique for *recycling* naughty little girls. It seems they suck out the entire contents of their brains, all those naughty little thoughts, and replace them with the National Curriculum and the Thoughts of Mabel Lucie Atwell.'

'I see you got the dents out of your van,' said Marmalade as Rufus strolled over and stood very close to it.

'All right, little girl, I can take a hint,' said Harry Hawk. 'I'm sure I'll catch up with you soon.' Smiling his horrible smile at Marmalade, he got quickly into his car, rolled up the window and drove away.

Rufus strolled off to see Jenny and Marmalade went into the house, where she found her father reading a letter from the Master of Goodness Gracious College.

'I can't understand this,' he said. 'It says here, because you and Rufus have been so bad and interesting beyond the call of duty, they're *sending you down.*'

'Yeah, that's right, Dad,' said Marmalade.

'Well, what are you doing here then? This isn't down, is it? This is sort of across, I'd have said. It's sideways.'

'It's *up*, if you look at a map,' said Mrs Atkins. 'I wish they *had* sent her down. I wish they'd sent her *right* down. I wish they'd sent her *down under*.'

'Here, that's an idea,' said Mr Atkins. 'I do happen to have some slightly iffy airline tickets. How would you like to go to Australia, Marmalade?'

'I wouldn't mind,' said Marmalade. 'I think I need to get away from Mr Hawk the Hooky Man.'

'What a brilliant idea!' shrieked Mrs Atkins. 'They *are* one-way tickets, I hope!'

'This is absolutely out of order,' said the Chief Steward, as the engines hummed and the plane warmed up for take-off. 'You cannot take a donkey in Business Class, madam.'

'Shut your cakehole, my good man, and bring us a glass of pop and a bag of oats,' said Marmalade. 'This isn't just any old donkey; this is Lord Rufus, an important diplomatic donkey who is travelling incognito to avoid publicity. Come here, cock.'

The Chief Steward bent down and Marmalade whispered in his ear: 'He's actually a *very important member* of the *Royal family*!'

'Cripes!' gasped the Chief Steward, who was

not only a bit of a snob but also a complete idiot. 'Terribly sorry, you Royal Highness. Don't worry, sire; your secret is safe with me. Brilliant disguise, sire; you certainly fooled me! Please accept my apologies! You're a donkey as far as I'm concerned, your Majesty, no danger!'

'Hee-*haw*!' said Rufus.

'Oh, brilliant, sire! Best donkey imitation I ever heard! Bag of oats coming up, sire, and one glass of pop for your . . . er . . .'

'Private detective, cock,' said Marmalade.

'Of course!'

Telling the snobby steward that Rufus was Royalty turned out to be rather a good idea. As soon as the plane landed at Sydney Airport, all sorts of airport big nobs crowded round and helped Marmalade and Rufus into a gold-plated trolley and wheeled them off to the VIP Lounge, where Rufus toyed with a plateful of asparagus and a salad of assorted leaves and Marmalade prowled about the room trying to look like a bodyguard.

The Governor of New South Wales arrived, a bit out of puff, and went down on one knee in front of Marmalade and Rufus.

'Rise, my good fellow,' said Marmalade. 'All mates here.'

'We was just wondering if you'd like to take a gander at the Test Match, sire,' said the Governor respectfully. 'Front row seats, free nosh, fair dinkum day out.'

'Hee-*haw*!' said Rufus.

'Sire says he would,' said Marmalade.

'Mind you, our boys are giving your boys a fearful hammering,' chuckled the Governor.

And they were.

Cricket, for those of you who haven't played it, is a terrible game, ninety per cent boredom and ten per cent terror. They play it with a nasty hard ball; when you are out you are out and you never get a second chance; and it is full of ridiculous rules and absurd names for the positions people stand in, such as *silly mid-off* or *square leg*. The most important games of cricket are called Test Matches, and England are always very keen to beat Australia in these Test Matches, but they hardly ever do.

When Marmalade and Rufus arrived at the Sydney Cricket Ground, Australia had made 424 runs for only 2 wickets, and Bruce Brawn and Brian Brown, the chief Australian batsmen, were knocking the ball all over the place. Grahame Glum, the England captain, his face as black as thunder, was muttering dire curses into his beard. The hot antipodean sun burned down so fiercely that players and spectators were fainting away. You would think that anyone sensible would pack it in and go and have an ice-cream, but England's honour was at stake. Grahame Glum trundled up and bowled another ball, and Brian Brown swung his bat in another mighty hit. The ball soared in the air, higher and higher. Two England fielders, rushing to get into position underneath it, collided with each other, cracked heads, and fell unconscious.

Then something extraordinary happened. With a loud creaking bray, Rufus rose from his seat and cantered lightly into the arena, kicking up his hooves. Raising himself on his hind legs, he reared up and caught the ball between his yellow teeth. To deafening applause, he galloped round the ground with it. The two batsmen were so astonished that they stopped where they were, in the middle of the pitch. Rufus galloped to the wickets, knocked off the bails, first at one end and then the other, and then sat down in the middle of the wicket, breathing heavily.

'HOWZAT???' yelled Marmalade.

The umpire lifted his hand, with one index finger erect. 'Out!' he said.

'Who's out?' growled Bruce Brawn.

'Both of you!' said the umpire. 'You're both run out!'

'You can't be run out by a flippin' *donkey*!' snarled Brian Brown, waving his bat menacingly.

'Substitute fielder, cock,' said Marmalade. 'He's twelfth man, and I'm thirteenth man.'

'If you think we're gettin' the bum's rush from a flippin' scruffy old animal like that . . . ' began Bruce Brawn, but then Rufus flashed his yellow teeth and began to paw the turf sending showers of earth over his shoulders and making the ground shake and tremble.

Bruce Brawn looked at Brian Brown.

'On the other hand, cobber,' he said in a rather quavery voice.

Brian Brown didn't say anything at all. He dropped his bat and started running very fast towards the pavilion, and Bruce Brawn dropped his bat too and followed hard on his heels. They had *nearly* reached the pavilion when Rufus caught up with them and chomped great big holes in the seat of their trousers. Then they ran up the steps, vainly attempting to cover their embarrassment, while Rufus strolled back to the middle of the pitch, with scraps of white cotton dangling from the corners of his mouth.

'I likes a little game of cricket,' he said to Grahame Glum. 'So does my little mate, young Marmalade there. So how about letting us have a bowl, eh?'

Graham Glum glowered. 'Cricket is a game for men, not for donkeys and girls,' he roared.

'Let 'em have a go!' yelled the crowd. 'They can hardly do worse than your lot!'

'Nice pair of trousers you got there, Mr Glum,' said Rufus. 'Nice bit of white cotton, nice chewy-lookin' buttons. I always says British trousers is far more tasty than the Australian variety.'

Grahame Glum knew how to take a hint. 'All right . . . er . . .'

'Atkins,' said Rufus. 'Ruthless Rufus Atkins, that's me.'

'All right, Atkins, you can have a go from the pavilion end. What do you bowl?'

'Donkey drops,' said Rufus. 'I bowls donkey drops, me.'

The new batsman, Bruce Brough, took guard, and Rufus blew on the ball and rubbed it hard on his leathery ginger backside until it shone like a new penny. Then he trundled slowly up to the wicket with the ball wedged in his front hoof, and tossed it high in the air. It seemed to hang there for minutes, shimmering and pulsating like a crimson ball of fire against the cruel brightness of the sky. Bruce Brough rubbed his eyes. He was dazzled. He was dizzy. Suddenly the ball was plummeting down on him and he swung his bat in a desperate effort and fell over backwards on the stumps.

'Howzat?' said Marmalade.

'OUT!' said the umpire.

Bruce Hogg was out the same way, and so was Bruce Bogg. Brian Brute knocked himself out and retired hurt. Bruce Brady, Bruce Grady and Bruce O'Dady were bowled. Bruce Binns and Bruce Minns were sent off for arguing with the umpire.

Australia were all out!

Grahame Glum led the England team back to the pavilion for lunch. 'So far so good,' he said. 'The donkey done well, I will say that. But it's not over yet, lads. We've still got over four hundred runs to make, and Bruce Brawn and Brian Brute are pretty fierce bowlers. Let's talk tactics.'

'We never talk tactics,' said Marmalade. 'Leave it to us, cock, and everything will be just fine. I'm off for a little snooze. It was hot in that sun and I'm really sleepy.'

'And I'm off for a stroll,' said Rufus. 'See you later, young Marmalade.'

Marmalade did feel sleepy, and really quite strange – Australian sun is very hot . . . maybe she'd had a bit too much of it. She found a nice comfortable-looking pile of old cricket pads in the corner, curled up on it and closed her eyes . . .

'Wake up, Marmalade! Pad up and get in there!' It was Grahame Glum, leaning over her, black beard a-bristle.

'What?' said Marmalade woozily. 'You're not putting me in first, are you?'

'No, last,' said the gloomy captain. 'You've slept through the entire innnings. We started off all right, but we've had another collapse, and that donkey of yours has disappeared completely.'

'How many runs do we need?' said Marmalade.

'A hundred and one,' said Glum miserably.

'Never mind, cock,' said Marmalade. 'It's only

a game, after all.' She strapped on some pads, put on a cap and picked up a bat, and stepped out of the pavilion into the blinding bright sunshine. The Australian crowd were shouting 'Finish her off, cobber!' and Bruce Brawn was tossing the ball from hand to hand with an evil glint in his eye.

Then from far away Marmalade heard an enormous 'Hee-*haw*!' and turned to see an amazing sight: Rufus had come back from his little stroll in the outback and had brought a team of kangaroos with him. With Rufus trotting in the lead, the kangaroos bounced solemnly around the perimeter of the pitch. Some of them were wearing their boxing gloves, and some of them had baby kangaroos in their pouches. Policemen and officials rushed on to the pitch to drive them out, but the kangaroos were having none of this: they had come to put themselves about, and they bounced all over the place, boxing the ears of any unfortunate policeman who came within reach. Soon the police and officials decided to take the sensible course and retreat, and the kangaroos all settled down in the front rows and got out their binoculars and their cans of Foster's lager.

Rufus strolled out to the wicket.

'You took your time, cock,' said Marmalade. 'What have you been up to?'

'Went walkabout,' said Rufus. 'I likes Australia. Fair dinkum time I been having, cobber.'

'Blimey!' said Marmalade. 'You're even talking Australian now.'

'Learnt it off the roos,' said Rufus.

'Well, look here,' said Marmalade. 'England's future is at stake again. It's all down to us. We're the last two in, and we've got to make a hundred and one runs!'

'No worries, mate,' said Rufus. 'Nice blokes, them kangaroos. They been showing me how to do the boomerang shot.'

'What's a boomerang shot?' said Marmalade.

Rufus told her, speaking in a low voice so that no one could hear. Then he pulled his cap down over his eyes, and the pair got ready to face the might of the Australian bowling.

Rufus had first strike. Brian Brawn took such a long run up to the wicket, he was just a dot in the distance when he started. Charging up like an express train, he let the ball fly from his hand like a rocket. Rufus took a swing, and the ball flew all the way to the boundary – where Bruce Brough was waiting to catch it.

'Oh, no!' yelled Marmalade.

But just as it seemed about to thud into his hands, the ball did something extraordinary – it looped the loop, then shot off in a completely different direction.

'Run!' said Rufus, and he and Marmalade ran up and down the pitch. Every time a fielder got near the ball, it changed direction, until eventually it trickled over the boundary.

'Boomerang shot,' said Rufus modestly. 'Learnt it off me mates.'

The Australians never recovered. They had no answer to the boomerang shot. The ball boomeranged all over the place and they were driven to distraction as they floundered after it, frequently cracking heads as they charged into each other. Marmalade scored fifty not out, and Rufus scored fifty-one not out. England had won the Test Match, thanks to Marmalade, Rufus and the age-old wisdom of the kangaroos.

Later that night, there was a huge party, with a good deal of bouncing round the billabong. The didgeridoos twanged far into the night, and the kangaroos sang 'Tie me down, sport! Tie me down!' while bouncing so high that no one had a chance of tying them down. Grahame Glum had a few tubes of lager, cheered up considerably, and spent most of the evening waltzing with a very nice kangaroo called Matilda under the shade of a coolibah tree. A few jolly swagmen turned up and offered Rufus the contents of their tucker-bags, which everyone thought was a very nice gesture. Round about midnight, Rufus and Marmalade did a few of their favourite songs and dances, which got the kangeroos very excited. Brian Brawn had a fight with a boxing kangaroo, and was knocked out in the third round.

All in all, it was one of the best parties Marmalade can remember going to, and back Down Under they still talk about it . . . and they still tell the story of how a skinny little girl and a scruffy ginger donkey changed the course of the strangest Test Match of all.

Marmalade on Ice

One morning not long after the strange events Down Under, Marmalade woke up in her own bed at home and looked out of the window. There was a lacy pattern of frost on the window panes that reminded her of Embroidery Classes at Hard Tack Hall and the day she had embroidered Mr Suckling-Pygge to the piano stool. She rubbed the pane clear and stared out. All the fields were under snow, there were fifteen centimetres of it covering Mr Atkins's Rolls-Royce, and the sheep all looked as if they'd been sent to the dry cleaners.

Her mother and father were still snoring in their beds, so Marmalade pulled on several layers of jumpers and coats, and her big yellow wellies, grabbed a few sausages and a handful of celery from the fridge, and walked over to the stable to see how poor old Rufus was getting on. Perhaps he would be shivering and pathetic from having spent the night in a draughty old shed.

But he wasn't. He was jumping about in the snow, rolling about on his back in it, kicking his legs in the air and hee-hawing like any daft young donkey. When he saw Marmalade he stopped rolling and hee-hawing and stood up, looking slightly embarrassed.

'I likes a bit of snow,' he said. 'Perks a donkey up, does a bit of snow. Good hard frost, this is. Might go down Kenilworth Abbey Fields, do a bit of skating, like.'

'*Skating?*' said Marmalade. 'Can you *skate?*'

'After a fashion,' said Rufus rather shiftily. 'I has a go, sort of thing.'

Marmalade went in and got her skates. She wasn't very good at skating, but she liked to have a go too. Last time she had tried it, she had been banned for life from Solihull Ice Rink for causing a major pile-up. That was two years ago, so she was a bit out of practice.

When Marmalade and Rufus got to Kenilworth Abbey Fields they found that plenty of people had had the same idea. People were tobogganing madly down the hill, some of them on proper toboggans, some of them on weird home-made sledges, some of them on teatrays and even old refuse sacks. The slope was very steep, with an icy stream at the bottom, and the people who couldn't steer very well (which was most of them) went crashing into it. Nobody seemed to mind very much. They're a mad lot in Kenilworth, and Marmalade and Rufus felt very much at home there.

They had a few goes at tobogganing on Marmalade's dad's roof rack. A roof rack makes a very good toboggan, especially if you grease it up with a pound or two of butter or low-fat spread, and if you can borrow a car seat or two you can have a real luxury five-star sledge. Unfortunately, Rufus was a little bit too heavy for the roof rack, especially when it went over the bumps at sixty miles an hour. Every time it landed, it bent it into ever more interesting shapes, and by the time Marmalade and Rufus had tried (and *nearly* succeeded) to make their toboggan leap right over the stream, it stopped looking like a roof rack at all, and looked more like an interesting piece of modern sculpture. Marmalade and Rufus looked at it dubiously.

'What's your dad going to say about that?' said Rufus.

'I expect he'll be dead pleased,' said Marmalade. 'Much more interesting than a roof rack, having a bit of genuine modern sculpture on your car roof. It'll probably get to be all the fashion, and he'll sell it for thousands and thousands of pounds. Come on; let's go skating.'

When they got to the lake, half the people were skating and the rest were laughing at a local beagle called Chowder, who was very determinedly trying to chase ducks across the ice. Every time he got up speed, he lost his balance, but instead of falling right over, he zoomed across the ice in a sitting-up position, facing backwards, with a totally baffled expression on his face. The ducks found it particularly amusing, and kept waddling and flapping up close to him to tempt him into having another go.

'Come on, young Marmalade,' said Rufus. 'Let's get amongst 'em. Let's put ourselves about a bit.' So they both took deep breaths and launched themselves out on to the ice.

At first, they were very rusty. Rufus did a couple of Chowders and skidded right across the lake on his bottom at forty miles an hour, while Marmalade tottered right round the edge of the lake, desperately trying to keep upright, and pulled down sixty-three spectators. But after a while they got into the swing of things, and Rufus started to skate suspiciously well, swooping out at an angle with his front hoof and tucking his rear hoof up behind him, and even doing fancy turns; and when the Kenilworth Silver Band struck up on the other side of the lake, he started to dance in time to the music. Marmalade scrabbled over the ice to catch up with him, and just managed to grab his mane to hold herself up, as he swooped and turned in graceful circles with a solemn, faraway expression on his face.

And now a strange thing happened – Marmalade found that when she was holding on to Rufus, she could balance, she could feel the way the skates wanted to go, she could really do it. All the people who had been laughing at the mad little girl and the crazy donkey stopped laughing and started to clap. It was really very strange indeed. Marmalade had never been very keen on dancing – except on rare occasions like

Kangaroo parties, it seemed to her a rather soppy occupation for a Bad Girl – but dancing on the ice with Rufus in the Abbey Fields was something else again. It was not soppy. It was all right. It was brilliant!

Suddenly a nasty sharp voice rang out across the frozen lake. 'Shouldn't you be in school, little girl?'

There on the bank was Harry Hawk . . . and this time he wasn't alone. He had a squad of government Hooky Men with him, armed with Truant Tridents like giant toasting forks, and huge Hooky nets made out of steel mesh . . . and behind him, Marmalade saw not only Harry Hawk's little black van, but another van, the big grey lorry from the Bad Girls Recycling Plant.

'Oh, Rufus!' wailed Marmalade. '*Now* what are we going to do?'

'Desperate situations call for desperate meas-ures,' said Rufus. 'Get on me back and hold tight, young Marmalade!' And with a huge 'Hee-*haw*!' he started to speed-skate around the edge of the frozen lake, with a mad grin on his face. He was going so fast that his shoes were sizzling and throwing off sparks. All the other skaters scattered and scrambled up on to the banks, but Harry Hawk smiled a nasty little smile and turned to his squad of Hooky Men.

'Ready with the nets and Truant Tridents, my brave boys!' he snarled.

The Hooky Men crept up with their nets and

tridents and lunged forward as Rufus and Marmalade hurtled past – but Marmalade grabbed hold of the edge of the net and hung on to it. The crowd gasped. All the Hooky Men grabbed hold of the other end of the giant net and braced themselves.

'Hold on tight, my brave boys, and we've got 'em cold!' grinned Harry Hawk, spitting on his hands. But ten government Hooky Men are no match for a ginger donkey at full stretch.

'Hee-*haw*!' went Rufus, and the whole gang of them got dragged on to the ice, tridents, net and all. They had no skates, and so they started to fall over straight away, and as Rufus skated faster and faster and in smaller and smaller circles, they became more and more tightly entangled in their own net. After ten more circuits they looked like nothing so much as a giant string bag of very knobbly old potatoes spinning round and round in the middle of the frozen lake, and all the people of Kenilworth were laughing and cheering fit to bust.

Rufus slowed his speed to a lazy glide and did a lap of honour, raising one front hoof to acknowledge the cheers of the crowd.

'Come on then, young Marmalade,' he said. 'Time to be going home, I reckon.'

When they got home, Rufus mooched off to tell his girlfriend Jenny about his exploits, and Marmalade went into the house, where she found a big fat man with a cigar talking to her mother and father.

'Ah, here she is, our little darling!' said Mr Atkins. 'Come on in, dear; don't be shy of the nice gentleman!'

Marmalade glared at him suspiciously. It was easy to tell when her dad was up to something. The big fat man, who was wearing a camel-hair overcoat and lots of jewellery, smiled a horrible smile at her, showing several gold teeth.

'This is Mr Arthur Bung,' said Mrs Atkins. 'He happened to see you in the Abbey Fields this morning.'

'Wasn't me,' said Marmalade. 'Some big girls done it and ran away. There were beagles involved as well. Me and Rufus never went near the place. Mistaken identity, cock. Hey, are those your teeth or did you swallow the crown jewels?'

Mr Bung smiled even more broadly. 'Witty too,' he said. 'But you got me wrong, Miss Atkins. I haven't come here to complain. I was very impressed with your performance with the donkey. Very impressed indeed.'

'Mr Bung's come to make you an offer,' said Mr Atkins.

'Yes, I have, my dear,' said Mr Bung. 'How would you like to be a novelty ice-dancer on the continent? With your, er, ginger confederate, of course.'

'I dunno,' said Marmalade. 'I've heard of

girls who went off to be novelty dancers on the continent, and were never heard of again, cock.'

'Yes! Yes!' shrieked Mrs Atkins excitedly.

'No need to worry, my little treasure,' said Mr Atkins. 'I am assured that Mr Bung here is absolutely trustworthy.'

'How much did he bung you?' said Marmalade.

'Three thous— a nominal sum, my love. It's your welfare that matters most to us; you know that.'

'Well,' said Marmalade, 'If it's that or school . . . yeah, why not? It might be a bit of fun.'

And it was. Marmalade and Rufus turned out to be a sensation all over Europe with their novelty ice-dancing, staying in posh hotels and putting themselves about from Helsinki to Vladivostok. One morning they were eating breakfast in bed in the VIP suite of the Chaliapin Hotel in Tomsk, when Mr Bung burst in with the most thrilling news of all.

'I got you a booking as cabaret and comedy relief at the Winter Olympics! You'll be seen on telly all over the world!'

But, as it turned out, that was only the half of it.

A lot of strange things happened at the Winter Olympics that year. Some of the most fancied competitors had to withdraw because of accidents. Masked mystery men kept turning up and whacking skaters in the leg. The Canadian champion got so dazzled by the sequins on his own trousers that he did a triple Lutz straight into the crowd, and seventeen people had to go to hospital. The British champions, Betty Bovril and Christopher Beans, were eliminated after the failure of one of their most spectacular moves. This was when Betty Bovril had to pick Christopher Beans up, whirl him round her head, and then toss him up in the air where he turned over twice before she caught him neatly on her bottom. Unfortunately, in the semi-finals, just as Betty tossed Christopher up she started wondering if she had turned the gas off before leaving England, and she completely forgot to stick her bottom out. Poor Christopher Beans landed on his head, making a nasty crack in the ice, and Bovril and Beans were out of the championship!

So it was that Marmalade and Rufus found themselves Britain's sole representatives in the ice-dancing championship, and their Back to Basics dancing style proved unusually popular. Some people called it British Grunge, because Marmalade and Rufus were so scruffy. No tights and sequins, glittery jackets and boleros for them: Marmalade skated in her old jumper and jeans, and Rufus went on as himself, with large fragments of mud clinging to his shaggy ginger coat. He wore his old cloth cap, his mane stood up in about six different directions at once, and he smelt very strongly of donkey.

'People seems to like this Back to Basics style,' he said, laughing his terrible wheezy creaky-gate laugh. 'Silly dang fools!'

Rufus was lolling at his ease in the front row, as he and Marmalade waited to go on in the finals of the ice-dance. The Russian champions, Kortakoff and Pusharova, were on the ice. Pusharova was tall and thin, with a short-skirted scarlet dress, and Kortakoff was even taller, and wore a feathered cap, black tights and glittery braces.

'They're good,' said Marmalade.

'Good but fancy,' said Rufus. 'I prefers something a bit hairier myself.'

The spangly Russians finished their routine to shrieks of delighted applause, and a lot of numbers flashed up on the scoreboard, mostly five point eights and five point nines, which are very high marks in ice dancing (the highest possible is a six which means perfection).

'That was your technical,' said Rufus knowledgeably. 'Next lot's your artistic.'

Up went another lot of figures. Again it was five point eights and five point nines, but there were one or two sixes this time.

'Ar,' said Rufus. 'Not bad skaters, them Russians.'

The loudspeakers boomed: 'And finally, representing the United Kingdom, Marmalade and Rufus Atkins!'

Before Marmalade had properly grasped what

was happening, she was on the ice, with the roar of the crowd in her ears, swooping around in great whirling circles and zig-zags and boomer-ang turns, balancing lightly with one hand in Rufus's shaggy old ginger mane. The crowd started to clap in time to the music, which was 'Who Wants to Be A Millionaire?' and suddenly Marmalade felt the words – her words and Rufus's special words – flooding back into her brain. They started to sing as they danced, Mar-malade high and raucous and Rufus gruff and wheezy, and this is what they sang:

Rufus: Who wants to wear a spangled suit?
Marmalade: I don't!
Rufus: Who wants to be all sweet and cute?
Marmalade: I don't!
Rufus: Who goes to parties in a pink velvet dress?
Marmalade: I never wear a dress! I like to look a mess!
Rufus: Who loves to ride in Daddy's car?
Marmalade: I don't!
Rufus: Who wants to be a movie star?
Marmalade: I don't!
Rufus: Who wants to be a beauty queen too?
Marmalade: Well, I don't!
Rufus: And I don't!
Marmalade and Rufus: 'Cos all we want is to stamp and shout and put ourselves about! Marmalade and Rufus! Rah! Rah! Rah!

The crowd were going hysterical by now, and

Marmalade and Rufus got a bit wild themselves: Rufus bared his yellow teeth in a mad grin as they swooped in huge circles round the perimeter, dragging people on to the ice to join in the dance. The whole rink was full of people dancing and jumping about and falling over, and rolling on top of each other and screaming with hysterical laughter, when suddenly Marmalade glimpsed Harry Hawk at the head of a hundred grim-looking little men. They were wearing helmets and ice-hockey outfits with EURO HOOKY TEAM written on their chests, and brandishing Ice-Hooky sticks, too, and they looked mean and cruel. Harry Hawk grinned his horrible grin.

'Little girl! Little girl! Shouldn't you be in school?'

Now ten Hooky Men with nets and tridents on a frozen lake in Kenilworth Abbey Fields is one thing, but a hundred Hooky Men with Ice-Hooky sticks at the Winter Olympics is another. Marmalade Atkins is a brave girl, but she has her limits.

'Help!' yelled Marmalade.

'Down here,' said Rufus. He led Marmalade down some dark steps, under the stadium. It was very dark, but Marmalade could make out a big control panel with lots of buttons and switches on it, and television screens showing all the different parts of the stadium.

'Try poking a few of them buttons,' said Rufus.

Marmalade pressed one of the buttons, and a picture of the ice rink came up on the screens, with all the people falling about on the ice, and Harry Hawk and his Hooky Men tripping each other up with their Hooky sticks.

'Hey, that's good,' said Marmalade. 'I wonder what that big red button does. Shall I try it?'

'Why not?' said Rufus

Marmalade pressed the big red button. Nothing seemed to be happening for a few seconds, then she stared at the screen.

'Hey!' she said. 'The ice is melting!'

It was too. All the skaters in spangly dresses and the rich spectators in their fur coats and the hundred Euro Hooky Men were stumbling about in wet slush . . . and then the first of them started to fall through, with a creak and a clatter and a plop.

'Let's go up and have a proper look,' said Rufus. By the time they got back up to the stadium it had turned into a giant swimming pool, full of thrashing splashing bodies.

'Synchronised swimming!' said Marmalade. 'Shall we join in?'

'I don't mind if I do, Marmalade Atkins,' said Rufus.